JOY *in the* COFFEE SEASON

Tilak Ponappa was born in the Nilgiri Hills and spent his formative years at The Lawrence School, Lovedale. He lived in America for several years, where he conducted research on the biochemistry, tissue culture and genetic engineering of plants, and has a PhD from The Ohio State University. He eventually moved back to India where he now lives with his wife on a coffee estate in Coorg (Kodagu), Karnataka, tending to his plants and assorted canine and feline friends. He comes from a long line of coffee and tea planters, and writes about life in this region in a humorous way.

Tilak Ponappa's earlier novel *Joy in Coorg* chronicled the often hilarious adventures of Joyappa, a coffee planter. *Joy in the Coffee Season* picks up the threads of Joyappa's life and describes his comical escapades in the picturesque hills of the Nilgiris and Coorg. Tilak Ponappa is also the author of *The Cougar*.

JOY *in the* COFFEE SEASON

TILAK PONAPPA

Published by
Rupa Publications India Pvt. Ltd 2024
7/16, Ansari Road, Daryaganj
New Delhi 110002

Sales centres:
Bengaluru Chennai
Hyderabad Jaipur Kathmandu
Kolkata Mumbai Prayagraj

Copyright © Tilak Ponappa 2024

This is a work of fiction. Names, characters, places and incidents are either the product of the author's imagination or are used fictitiously and any resemblance to any actual person, living or dead, events or locales is entirely coincidental.

All rights reserved.
No part of this publication may be reproduced, transmitted, or stored in a retrieval system, in any form or by any means, electronic, mechanical, photocopying, recording or otherwise, without the prior permission of the publisher.

P-ISBN: 978-93-6156-386-7
E-ISBN: 978-93-6156-368-3

First impression 2024

10 9 8 7 6 5 4 3 2 1

The moral right of the author has been asserted.

Printed in India
This book is sold subject to the condition that it shall not, by way of trade or otherwise, be lent, resold, hired out, or otherwise circulated, without the publisher's prior consent, in any form of binding or cover other than that in which it is published.

For Bollachi

My grandmother, whose eclectic literary tastes were an inspiration to many

Contents

Preface / ix

Author's Note / xi

1. Joy in the Hills / 1

2. Joy in School / 31

3. The Killjoys / 74

4. Good News! / 91

5. Dental Problems / 100

6. The Dinner Party / 109

7. Joy in the Coffee Season / 135

Acknowledgements / 175

Glossary / 177

*P*reface

Joyappa, or 'Joy' to his wife, is a planter based in Coorg (Kodagu), a small district in the southern state of Karnataka. Joyappa is married to Susheela—daughter of a much decorated, retired army General and his somewhat intimidating wife. Joyappa and Susheela have a son, Thimmaiah (also known as Timmy), who is a student at a prestigious boarding school in the Nilgiri Hills of Tamil Nadu. Susheela is very attached to her son and misses him greatly when he is away at school.

As Joyappa's maturity leaves something to be desired, Susheela is continually striving to keep him on the 'straight and narrow' and mould him into a responsible husband and parent. Unfortunately for her, while Joyappa *has* grown, most of the progress has been physical, as evidenced by his enlarged girth. Despite Susheela's best efforts, Joyappa's sense of responsibility resembles that of a flighty teenager.

Joyappa's behaviour is sometimes so immature that Susheela is forced to resort to deception, bribery and even practical jokes, to encourage him to adhere to his diet and to keep his vices in check. Regardless of her attempts to reform him, Joyappa—often aided and abetted by his equally irresponsible friends—invariably finds himself in trouble.

One of Joyappa's goals is to travel abroad to visit a couple of like-minded friends. To earn money for an exotic holiday, he works hard during the 'coffee season', which culminates in the annual coffee harvest. Joyappa works diligently during this period and tries to discharge all his duties in a responsible manner. However, the gruelling schedule, his hare-brained schemes, immature friends and an inability to resist temptation result in hilarious and unforeseen consequences.

This volume of Joyappa's adventures starts with Susheela dragging her reluctant husband to Timmy's school to witness and participate in the elaborate Annual Day functions. Predictably, things do not go as planned. Much to Susheela's chagrin, Joyappa dances to the beat of a different drum and manages to rock the very foundations of a prestigious institution.

Author's Note

As Joyappa stumbles through life, I trust his escapades become a source of amusement. I also hope that in some small way, the brief description of the coffee 'season' gives readers an appreciation for the challenges faced by planters in the hills of southern India.

In general, many difficulties encountered by Joyappa are common to farmers everywhere. In spite of taking great care to carry out agricultural operations in a timely manner, weather often plays spoilsport. Extreme temperatures, extended periods of drought and excessive rainfall at critical periods of plant development are devastating to crop yield. Deforestation, rapid and unplanned urbanization, leading to the loss of animal habitat, are additional factors that adversely affect agriculture. Sadly, these conflicts often lead to destruction of crops and the tragic loss of life and limb of both humans and animals.

Despite these challenges, living close to nature and growing plants has a charm all of its own. So, I hope young people armed with innovative ideas and enthusiasm find satisfaction in agricultururral pursuits while preserving the biodiversity of their region.

1

Joy in the Hills

Joyappa gazed at the magnificent panorama before him. He was lounging in a comfortable armchair on the verandah of a colonial-era bungalow approximately 8,000 feet above mean sea level, just outside the town of Ooty, in the Nilgiris.

The morning was cool, and as the mist gradually lifted, it revealed more and more of the mountains nearby and the valley below. Joyappa could see the mountainsides to his left covered with manicured tea bushes forming a lush green carpet with reddish mud roads winding through the plantations. A couple of silver-coloured factories, used to process tea leaves, gleamed as if kissed by the early morning sun. The mountains to Joyappa's right displayed assorted vegetation, including eucalyptus, pine, rhododendron and azalea. Some stark, intimidating peaks of glossy black rock protruded from the edges of the valley. Narrow streams and waterfalls dotted the landscape as they gurgled down to feed a clear, swift river that flowed to the distant plains.

Joyappa was in good spirits. The delicate fragrance of a steaming cup of high-grown tea wafted up to his hairy nostrils. He picked up a crisp biscuit, dipped it in his tea and placed the softened substance in his mouth. Inevitably, a chunk of the remaining biscuit broke off, rapidly sank to the bottom of the cup and settled there. Joyappa sipped the tea noisily. Before the cup got empty, Abraham, the butler, magically materialized before him and filled it with fresh hot tea. Joyappa smiled with gratitude, nodded in appreciation and consumed a few more biscuits using his preferred technique. When the cup was nearly empty, he tipped his head back and let the soggy mess at the bottom of the cup slide down his throat. He was glad his wife wasn't present to chastise him for his poor table etiquette.

Susheela had left early in the morning and was likely to be away for most of the day. She had planned a trek through a *shola*, or tropical montane forest, with several others who shared her love of the outdoors. Before leaving, she had instructed the bungalow's cook and butler to serve Joyappa a simple breakfast of oat porridge, one slice of papaya and a cup of tea—*nothing else*. While Susheela's directions were motivated by Joyappa's high cholesterol levels and burgeoning waistline, this sort of restrictive diet did not appeal to Joyappa, *especially* when he was on holiday.

Joyappa had cleverly circumvented the problem by slipping the staff of the bungalow a substantial sum of money. For good measure, he had sweetened the deal with a couple of bottles of rum carefully hidden in the tool compartment of his car.

As the aroma of the illicit breakfast diffused out to the verandah, Joyappa's salivary glands diligently responded while he rubbed his hands together in anticipation. Abraham, clad in his spotless white tunic topped with a matching turban, carried out a large tray with the much-awaited meal. He quietly placed the plates of food on the table beside Joyappa and discreetly returned inside the bungalow.

Joyappa sat up and 'went to work'. He tore into the cook's high-calorie creations like a ravenous jackal. Fried eggs, with gooey yolks, were supplemented with crisp bacon, sausages and ham. The plant kingdom was also well represented by tomatoes fried in bacon grease, deep fried potato wedges and thick slices of home-made bread slathered with marmalade and butter. Abraham, who had witnessed his share of remarkable sights in his many decades of service, was flabbergasted as he discreetly observed Joyappa from behind a curtain in the living room. Joyappa enjoyed every mouthful of his meal as he devoured everything that had been served. He briefly considered licking the remains of bacon grease and yolk directly off his plate and the serving dishes. Fortunately, Abraham's appearance with a pot of steaming coffee caused him to jettison the plan.

After washing down his breakfast with several cups of excellent filter coffee, Joyappa moved to a comfortable rocking chair on the verandah and made an effort to read the sports page of the newspaper. But his full stomach, the morning sun, the gentle movement of the rocking chair and the soothing buzz of a bumblebee caused him to fall into a comfortable slumber.

The reason Joyappa found himself in Ooty warrants an explanation. Joyappa lived in the little district of Coorg, located in the Western Ghats of Karnataka, where he managed the family's coffee plantation. After the annual harvest, Joyappa, along with his wife, Susheela, had spent a week in the plains of Mysore, where they attended a family wedding that was held in a stately royal palace. Susheela had worked hard on the arrangements for the function. The event was a grand success.

Predictably, with Susheela in charge of organizing the wedding, every aspect had been carefully considered in excruciating detail. Just as predictable was Susheela's fatigue that followed her extensive exertions. Joyappa, too was exhausted—mostly from witnessing Susheela's efforts. The sweltering heat of Mysore, too much rich food, liquor and dancing also contributed to his weariness in no small measure.

Soon after the wedding, Joyappa and Susheela departed for the Nilgiris, also known as the 'Blue Mountains'. As they crossed Karnataka's state boundary into Tamil Nadu, and began their ascent into the hills, the air became perceptibly cooler and fragrant with the scent of eucalyptus and pine.

Joyappa started to feel a lot better. Susheela also seemed more relaxed as she smiled at Joyappa for the first time in ages. She patted his shoulder affectionately as he drove up the winding road. However, the physical contact was fleeting, as she abruptly recoiled upon touching Joyappa's sweat-soaked shirt. Discreetly, she dried her hands on a paper towel (after applying a little hand sanitizer that she kept in the glove box precisely for such occasions).

Their son, Timmy, was enrolled in an exclusive school in Ooty, the beautiful hill station in the upper reaches of the Nilgiris. The Annual Day was a major event on the school calendar. During the week preceding the special day, the students were required to participate in various activities that showcased the institution's reputation as one of the premier schools in the country.

This year, the school had a new headmaster who decided that parents needed to be more involved in the 'build up' leading to the Annual Day. As the school did not permit students to reside off-campus, the teachers rarely got an opportunity to interact with the parents. The system had been in effect since the founding of the institution over a century before and had worked well to curtail parental interference in the day-to-day functioning of the school. The headmaster's new venture was designed to foster parent-teacher interaction, and, more importantly, to get the well-heeled parents to loosen their purse-strings and donate generously to the school.

Susheela wholeheartedly supported the new policy. Any opportunity to be near their son typically elicited an enthusiastic response from her. In contrast, Joyappa exhibited no desire to participate in any of the activities. Although Joyappa liked Ooty, he didn't particularly want to spend his free time with other parents or his son's teachers. Throughout his own lacklustre, and often troubled, academic career, he had consistently tried to avoid any kind of teacher. He saw no reason to alter this guiding principle.

Joyappa had made every effort to evade the visit to Ooty. He even lied to Susheela that he couldn't possibly make the journey as he had developed a severe case of haemorrhoids—knowing she was unlikely to check the veracity of his claim. His guess about Susheela avoiding a physical examination turned out to be right, but she had easily seen through the falsehood.

Susheela masterfully and cunningly countered with remedies for his imaginary problem. She told him that he would have to endure an exclusively vegetarian diet of sprouts, lettuce and overripe bananas for a minimum of six weeks. She also announced that during this period, he would no longer be allowed to sit in his favourite armchair; instead, he would have to park himself on the inflated inner tube of a scooter tyre. Joyappa was horrified. In his opinion, Susheela's planned treatment was at par with being waterboarded or subjected to some unspeakable medieval torture.

Joyappa was a beaten man, but he had his pride. To save

face, he waited for one whole day before announcing that he had recovered completely from his ailment and would indeed accompany Susheela on the trip.

For their stay in Ooty, Susheela had rented a charming heritage house that came with a resident cook, butler, housekeeper and gardener. Upon reaching the bungalow, Joyappa had to acknowledge that she had done a fine job of choosing their accommodation.

A few hours after his substantial breakfast, Joyappa woke up in the rocking chair, feeling refreshed. He yawned, stretched and stared fixedly at something in the valley below. He proceeded to do a fine job of imitating a log, albeit a slightly misshapen one with a bulge in the centre.

Meanwhile, Susheela breezed into the house, had a quick shower and stepped on to the verandah. Joyappa sensed her presence from the delicate floral perfume she favoured but could not summon the energy to even move his eyes, much less turn around to greet her.

'Hi, Joy,' Susheela said cheerfully, as she bent down to give him a peck on the cheek. Despite the long trek she had undertaken in the morning, she looked fresh as a daisy.

'Oh, hello,' Joyappa said, barely moving his lips. After the morning's gluttony, he was feeling too comfortable in his inert state to even lift a finger.

Susheela sniffed the air and said, 'Do you smell cigarette smoke?'

'Nope,' said Joyappa.

'I hope you haven't been smoking, Joy.'

'Nope. Remember, I quit ages ago,' Joyappa lied confidently, hoping that the butts he had flung off the verandah were well-concealed in the vegetation below.

'Must be the gardener or someone else then,' said Susheela. 'I must have a word with the staff. I've got to explain that it is an awful habit, an absolute waste of their hard-earned money and a serious health hazard as well.'

'True. But it could have been someone down in the valley,' said Joyappa, slightly worried that the staff may have seen him puffing away. He hadn't had a chance to bribe the gardener or the housekeeper yet, so they could very well squeal to Susheela. He resolved to grease their palms at the earliest opportunity.

'Joy, do you honestly think that the smell of tobacco would drift all the way up here from several hundred feet below?' Susheela asked sharply.

Without waiting for a response, she proceeded to update Joyappa about the various activities planned for the parents by the School Board in the coming week. 'The cross-country race is scheduled tomorrow. This year, it is open to the parents and teachers who want to participate, as well as the senior students, of course. You better not enter, Joy. I am a little concerned after your last medical exam.'

'Okay, if you say so,' Joyappa grunted, trying not to overtly express the relief he felt at avoiding a gruelling run.

'I plan to participate in the race. It should be a lot of fun and a good workout. I'll be out of here before you are up since they have scheduled an early start.'

'Okay,' Joyappa grunted again, as his eyes gleamed in anticipation at the possibility of another massive breakfast.

Susheela went on to explain that the Variety Entertainment Programme would be held on the day after the race. The Drama

Department would present numerous performances, including short skits by the younger children, and more elaborate shows by the senior students. Not to be outdone, the Music Department would also present a variety of recitals, with focus on Western and Indian classical music. The school play was the pièce de résistance. The play was to be a collaborative effort by both drama and music departments, and much effort had been expended to ensure that the production would be of the highest quality. In addition, at the headmaster's insistence, the parents had agreed to put up a short production just before the school play.

'Joy, I need to go shopping for some new clothes for the parents' skit. One of the parents is a well-known thespian from Mumbai. She was so warm and friendly to me. We struck up a conversation this morning on the trek, and she insisted that she has just the perfect part for me.'

Joyappa sat bolt upright. He turned pale and his eyes assumed saucer-like proportions.

Taken aback at the sudden movement, Susheela frowned. A moment later, the light dawned on her. She smiled and clarified. 'She's a famous stage actor, Joy.'

Joyappa felt an enormous sense of relief to know that Susheela would be subjected only to dramatic, rather than Sapphic instruction. He resumed his imitation of misshapen timber and said, quite untruthfully, 'Oh, I *knew* that, Susheela. I just thought I saw a rock bee getting ready to sting you.'

It slowly became clear that as Susheela was to be in the parents' skit, and Timmy had a role in his class play, Joyappa was expected to be in the audience. He winced slightly upon hearing this.

Thus far, Joyappa had not heard anything particularly

alarming. He just hoped to completely avoid participating in any of the activities.

Susheela continued to outline the rest of the schedule. She explained that the next event would be the science exhibition, which would feature elaborate posters and presentations by the students.

'Timmy will be presenting some of his projects. So, we both need to attend the exhibition,' Susheela announced. Joyappa winced again, this time with enough vigour to cause his belly to wobble. Fortunately, Susheela didn't notice.

The Department of Physical Education had organized a gymnastics and yoga display. Joyappa was, however, neither required to be present nor was he expected to be at the synchronized swimming show arranged for the same evening. Joyappa smiled. He thought he might be able to sneak away for a night on the town.

He listened placidly. A cricket match between the parents and the school team—consisting of teachers and senior students— was also scheduled. However, when Susheela casually mentioned that she had requested Joyappa's name be included on the parents' team, Joyappa's body jerked violently and his eyes widened. Again, Susheela appeared not to notice.

Joyappa had played hockey in his youth with some distinction. He was not averse to watching cricket, but, with all the confusing rules he couldn't remember and the eerie white attire that made him think of a funeral, he detested actually playing the sport. He also did not enjoy playing with weird bowlers who smeared saliva and sweat on the ball before rubbing it across their nether regions. Additionally, he found most bowling actions distasteful as they brought to mind the flapping of spastic water birds.

'As you know, the main event on the Annual Day is the parade,' Susheela continued. 'Obviously, we will have to be there. I'm really excited, as Timmy is in the marching band, an integral part of the parade. As always, the chief guest will be a highly accomplished person and I am looking forward to an inspiring speech,' Susheela chimed in, oblivious of Joyappa's misery.

Susheela further informed him that a 'social' had been organized for the teaching staff, senior students and parents.

'What's a social?' Joyappa asked nervously.

'It's just a formal dinner and dance, Joy,' Susheela said reassuringly. 'After all the activity on the Annual Day, I guess it is a chance to relax and have a bit of fun in the evening. Every parent is expected to attend, of course. I'm sure you will enjoy it,' she added.

This was too much for Joyappa. He jumped out of the rocking chair and yelled with his characteristic eloquence, 'Susheela, I'm not! I can't! I won't!'

'What do you mean, Joy?' Susheela enquired patiently.

'I've not objected to any of your requests this week. I must admit that you have involved me in more foolish activities than I ever expected. But this is the limit. I cannot take anymore! I am NOT spending an evening being polite and dancing with boring teachers, pimply teenagers and pompous parents, Susheela.'

'Come on, Joy,' said Susheela, soothingly.

'Nope,' countered Joyappa, as he stuck out his chin obstinately.

Realizing from long experience that only bribery would work, Susheela said, 'Okay, Joy. Here's the deal. If you attend the Variety Entertainment Programme, participate in the cricket match, be at the dinner and dance and behave yourself during the entire week, you can have a whole weekend with your pals at a place of your choosing.'

'Hmm,' considered Joyappa, as the wheels began to turn in his head. 'Make it four days. In Thailand.'

'Fine, four days. But *not* Thailand,' Susheela negotiated firmly. She knew that bailing out Joyappa and his irresponsible cronies from trouble in a distant land could be difficult.

'What do you have against Thailand? I want to vacation in another country, or I start walking back home tomorrow morning,' threatened Joyappa, obstinately.

'Come on, Joy. Be reasonable,' Susheela pleaded.

Joyappa thought for a moment, and said, 'I am not compromising on this. I insist that it be an overseas trip. If not Thailand, it *must* be Goa.'

Susheela was a bit puzzled, but Joyappa's statements were often enigmatic. She quickly agreed, 'Very well, Joy. Have it your way. Goa it is.'

Joyappa smirked. He was pleased with his ability to negotiate.

Just then, Abraham rang the gong and Susheela said, 'Time for lunch, Joy.'

Joyappa puffed out his chest as it was rare for him to win an argument with Susheela. He strutted into the dining room behind her.

However, the pride he felt was short-lived. Susheela turned to Joyappa and remarked with a sweet smile, 'You are having a really healthy meal, Joy. Thanks to all the nutritious vegetables they produce in the Nilgiris, the cook has prepared a salad with lettuce, sprouted chickpeas, radishes and bell peppers topped with a vinegar dressing. I've requested him to supplement the meal with boiled cabbage, Brussels sprouts and broccoli. You can wash it all down with a freshly prepared Momordica drink as well.'

Joyappa almost backed out of the room. He wondered if Susheela believed he was a goat. He then consoled himself that even if the vegetables were bland, at least the drink sounded interesting.

'Oh! I forgot to mention,' Susheela continued. 'We are expected to have tea in the school lawns this evening. It will be a great opportunity to meet the other parents, teachers and students,' she added as if to rub salt into his wound.

Joyappa was not in a good mood. He believed that Susheela had deliberately played a cruel prank on him at lunch. He had managed to eat the salad and the other bland, boiled vegetables in anticipation of the Momordica drink that Susheela had requested. Given its unusual name, he felt it was some sort of exotic cocktail. He hastily forced down the last Brussels sprout and grabbed the glass. He quickly swallowed half of its contents, hoping to wash away the awful taste of cruciferous vegetables. It took him a moment to realize that he had chugged down the most bitter (or was it *the bitterest?*) liquid he had ever had the misfortune to consume.

As Joyappa choked and spluttered, Susheela smiled the most angelic smile imaginable and remarked, 'Joy, did you know that the Latin name for bitter gourd is *Momordica charantia*? Would you like some more? It's good for your many ailments, you know.'

Joyappa pointedly ignored Susheela for most of the afternoon. As usual, she seemed largely unaffected by this behaviour. In fact, she was so anxious to see their son that Joyappa's grumpy demeanour did not even seem to register with her.

Later that afternoon, Joyappa and Susheela drove down the

narrow mountain road from the bungalow that passed through the quaint little town of Ooty. After negotiating a winding tar road, they reached the imposing gates leading to Cold Mountain Academy. Susheela produced a pass. The gatekeeper gave it a quick look, saluted smartly and invited them to enter.

Cold Mountain Academy was one of the premier schools in the country. Its alumni had distinguished themselves in various fields, including the military, industry, literature, science, art and music. In fact, one could name any discipline and be certain that a 'Mountaineer' had reached the summit in the field.

The campus was magnificent. In a country where land was at a premium, the campus spanned several hundred acres of prime property.

The driveway leading to the main school building was impressive. The juniper hedges on either side of the road were freshly trimmed and the lush green lawns perfectly complemented the numerous beds of colourful annuals that swayed in the gentle breeze. Various shrubs and strategically placed potted plants and the faint fragrance of eucalyptus leaves added to the ambience. The imposing school buildings, constructed over a century before by master craftsmen, stood majestically in this picturesque setting.

The overall effect was quite stunning. Even though they had visited the school on numerous occasions previously, Susheela felt the gardener and his crew had outdone themselves this time. She involuntarily gasped and said, 'Oh Joy! Doesn't everything look so lovely?'

Joyappa grunted. He wasn't in the mood to respond. His taste buds and innards were still shell-shocked from lunch. Consequently, his mood was decidedly sour; although 'bitter' perhaps would be a more accurate description of his disposition.

He thought that the astronomical school fees they paid for Thimmaiah could have certainly been put to better use than for the growth and maintenance of grass, flowers and hedges.

At the parking lot, a friendly, well-groomed girl, in the uniform of a prefect, greeted and guided them to the Quadrangle, where the headmaster was to address them in a few minutes. Several parents and the teaching staff had already assembled, and the buzz of polite conversations filled the air.

As scheduled, in a brief address, the headmaster welcomed the parents to the school for the Annual Day. He made a subtle suggestion that to remain one of the best educational institutions in the country, the school needed additional facilities, including a new computer lab, a plant tissue culture facility, two squash courts, an Olympic-sized swimming pool (heated, of course) and nine more holes added to the existing nine-hole golf course which would nicely meet the institution's immediate requirements. Further, he claimed, it pained him greatly to announce that considering the increase in operating costs the fees would *have* to be raised. Finally, with a smile (that to Joyappa's jaundiced eye seemed oily and ingratiating) the headmaster added that donations from parents would be much appreciated.

Joyappa was becoming angrier by the minute. He considered—not for the first time—how much money he could have saved if his son had attended a local school. Timmy would have received a reasonably decent education and Joyappa could have taught him to play hockey, shoot straight and fish. After all, beyond being able to read a newspaper and count to a thousand, what was the point in filling these kids' heads with more and more meaningless information?

Joyappa was perplexed as to why there was a round of applause following the headmaster's speech. He was taken aback and felt somewhat betrayed when he noticed that even Susheela was clapping vigorously. As the headmaster began to circulate amongst the parents, Susheela explained to Joyappa that he had quit his career as a corporate bigwig to live in the pristine environment of the Nilgiris and take Cold Mountain Academy to greater glory.

Several waiters serving pastries and tea began to make their way through the Quadrangle. When Joyappa reached for a particularly tempting slice of chocolate cake, Susheela quickly grabbed his arm in an apparent (and completely disingenuous) display of affection. Consequently, he was restricted to sipping a cup of unsweetened black tea, while watching others happily stuffing their faces with the finest confections from the school bakery.

Eventually, the headmaster made his way towards Susheela and Joyappa. He looked surprisingly young and slim, with delicate, boyish features that many women found attractive. Joyappa scowled at him as he thought to himself: *This is the twit who plans to increase the school fees and is responsible for forcing me to participate in lame, humiliating activities.*

The headmaster introduced himself as he took Susheela's hand, bowed low and said, 'Charmed, I'm sure.'

Susheela blushed prettily and giggled like a schoolgirl. This simpering irked Joyappa even further. When the headmaster turned towards him with a smile, Joyappa took the somewhat soft, manicured hand in his and squashed it in a vice-like grip. Admittedly, it was an immature action. Joyappa's numerous frustrations caused him to exert even more pressure as he shook the poor man's hand vigorously. The Headmaster—a Mr Rao, Raja or Roger (Joyappa couldn't quite recall his name)—flushed visibly, his smile faded and little beads of perspiration appeared on his forehead. When Joyappa finally let go of his hand, he scurried away without a backward glance.

Susheela, who was hoping to have a long discussion with the headmaster, was perplexed at this abrupt departure and said, 'That's strange, Joy. Why did he leave so suddenly? I wonder if he took ill.'

'He's probably a busy man. Lots of pressure, I'm sure,' said Joyappa, who was now in a much better mood.

'I suppose you are right. He seems really nice. I would have loved to spend more time with him. You do know he attended Eton, don't you?'

In Joyappa's opinion, the young man hadn't 'eaten' enough and could do with some meat on his bones. Wisely, however, he kept his counsel.

After tea, the parents were finally permitted to meet their children. Timmy ran up to his parents. He was a bespectacled, thin, diffident boy. He had grown since Joyappa and Susheela had last seen him, and a few fine hairs seemed to have sprouted above his upper lip.

'Hello, son,' said Joyappa, with a smile.

'Hi, Dad,' said the boy, awkwardly, before turning to his mother.

Susheela and Timmy then clung to each other like limpets. Soon, mother and son began to kiss each other with affection.

Joyappa could hear Susheela whisper, 'Oh, my baby. How I've missed you!'

Timmy responded with, 'Mummy, I have missed you more!'

Embarrassed, Joyappa was compelled to turn away from this very public display of affection. As he did so, he happened to see a couple of boys and a group of snooty-looking girls pointing and giggling at the spectacle.

Although Joyappa understood that in their place, he too might be tempted to point and giggle, he had to be loyal to his family. So, he glared menacingly at the youngsters, stroked his moustache and growled, 'What are you kids looking at? Get a move on!'

The students turned pale, looked away and quickly scurried out of the Quadrangle. Joyappa felt quite pleased with himself.

Early the following morning, before Joyappa stirred from his sleep, Susheela drove to the school campus. Clad in shorts and a tank top, she made her way to the stables where the participants of the cross-country race had been asked to assemble. Ten boys and a dozen girls, known to be the school's best long-distance racers, were already present there.

Susheela knew that even completing the race was going to be an uphill task. The air at that altitude was thin, she was not acclimatized and the students were much younger and possibly more athletic than her. Yet, she resolved to do her best.

With a quarter of an hour to go before the start of the race, Susheela decided to stretch. It was precisely at this point that the nature of the event changed and caused a shift in its outcome. It must be noted at the outset that Susheela was blessed with an incredibly attractive physique. Further, regular exercise, a careful diet and good genes had conspired to produce a figure of extremely pleasing proportions.

When Susheela sat on the grass outside the stables, and twisted her body into a yoga asana, she attracted the gaze of some male students selected for the race. These were teenagers with raging hormones who, not unexpectedly, stopped their warm-up session and stared at Susheela. Soon, other boys noticed her, and all but one of them, who happened to be short-sighted, began to observe her warm-up routine. When Susheela stood up and touched her toes, revealing long, shapely legs, several older men too became part of the audience. Susheela, however, remained focussed on her routine and oblivious to the effect she was causing.

Eventually, the starting gun fired and Susheela set off with her long, graceful stride along with the other competitors. From the stables, the runners were expected to skirt the cemetery, climb the steep Ibex Hill, pass through a section of the golf course thick with gorse bushes, run through the arboretum, descend a rocky slope, cut through a marshy area, climb a grassy hillock and reach the finish line in front of the headmaster's residence.

The course was well marked, and gruelling; the slopes of the hills were steep and the footing varied from hard, rocky surfaces to wet, muddy areas. The rarefied atmosphere in the mountains also made it particularly hard for those used to running at lower altitudes.

Occasionally, the path became so narrow that participants had to run in single file. In the open areas, they were able to run together in larger groups. Susheela observed that regardless of the location, she was always running with several boys in her vicinity. They constantly jockeyed for position, with most of them attempting to locate themselves just behind her.

Two of the normally sure-footed boys tripped and slipped off the path as they climbed the Ibex Hill. They took nasty tumbles and were unable to continue the race. The remaining boys didn't stop to help. Instead, they closed in further behind Susheela, seemingly hypnotized by her steady rhythmic movements while making her way up the hill. As they ran through the golf course, one of the boys charged into a spiny gorse bush and ripped open his calf. He was tough; he immediately tore off a piece of his jersey, bound his wound and gamely limped after Susheela. However, the injury had slowed him down considerably, and he was effectively eliminated.

As the runners approached Cold Mountain Arboretum, a passing shower drenched them, soaking their clothes and cooling down their bodies. Two of Susheela's jogging companions, trailing behind her immediately ramped up their pace and ran past her. While running between tightly spaced trees, they kept glancing behind at Susheela for some reason. The outcome was predictable. Being distracted, one of them crashed into a eucalyptus tree and was unable to continue; the other collided with a ponderosa pine and passed out.

While Susheela was finding the going tough, Joyappa was also struggling—but with a challenge of a different kind. He had decided to have a South Indian breakfast, and Abraham had just brought him his seventh buttered masala dosa from the kitchen. The first six had gone down quite smoothly, but Joyappa was disappointed to find that there was no more sambar in which he could dunk the dosa. He was a little upset, but what is life without hardship? So, he stoically ate the last dosa by using the cook's spicy coconut chutney for lubrication, before washing it all down with a pot of coffee.

Meanwhile, just as Susheela and her rapidly dwindling entourage had reached the bottom of the rocky declivity, she tripped over a loose stone and fell forward. As she slid down, the reaction from the remaining boys was immediate and in stark contrast to their response to the misfortunes of their fellow students. They helped her up, tore off pieces of their shirts and bound her bleeding knee. Susheela was touched; figuratively as well.

'Thank you so much, boys,' she said gratefully. When she smiled through her discomfort at her teenaged helpers, they were well and truly smitten. Consequently, Susheela had effectively ensured their willingness to carry her all the way to the finish line, if the need arose.

Fortunately, Susheela's injuries, though painful, were not severe. When she recommenced the race with her solicitous helpers, there were just five people ahead of them. Leading the pack was the myopic boy, who, unlike his colleagues, remained undistracted; his familiarity with the course allowed him to stay ahead despite his poor vision. He was followed by a triathlete from Mumbai, the CEO of a big corporation, whose daughter studied at the academy. A girl who had won the Nilgiris interschool mini marathon was in third place, followed by the school track coach, a former state middle-distance champion. A girl who had won the metric mile in the inter-house games was trailing the coach in fifth position.

Susheela gained momentum after getting through the slushy wetlands. She found her second wind and was able to overtake one of the girls as she ran up the grassy slope. When she closed in on the track coach, and attempted to pass him, he moved across to block her. Susheela's entourage did not take kindly to this move. One of the boys drew near the coach and tripped him with a deftly placed foot, an action unobserved by anyone else. The poor man fell and went rolling and partly sliding down the hillock.

Susheela was completely worn out by the time she crossed the finish line in front of the headmaster's house. Exhausted, she was content to have just finished the race. After having gathered her breath somehow, Susheela was proud to learn that she had been placed second among girls and had secured a surprising fourth overall.

Once he had limped over the finish line in fifteenth position, the track coach was surprised and acutely disappointed to find that the boys on whom he had pinned his hopes to win had performed so poorly. He resigned himself for the inevitable tongue-lashing from the headmaster. He was also puzzled because in all his years of competitive racing, he had never once fallen down during a race. 'Perhaps, I am getting too old for this strenuous stuff,' he reasoned with himself.

Susheela walked over to the boys who had assisted her, and after hugging the lads and bestowing them with a high-wattage smile, she said, 'Thanks so much for helping me, boys. That was incredibly kind of you.'

'It was our pleasure, Ma'am,' one of them managed to respond. The others remained tongue-tied, and just smiled. Politely holding their sweatshirts in front of them, some of them secretly resolved never to launder their T-shirts!

The following morning, despite being sore and slightly injured after the strenuous race, Susheela was excited to take part in the entertainment programme. Amidst all the activities, she had managed to squeeze in a couple of rehearsals for the skit. She explained to Joyappa over breakfast that she was to play a model and sashay down a catwalk in a silk gown and high heels. Joyappa nodded, smiled and pretended to be interested as she chattered on about the plot of the skit and her role in it.

Joyappa even made a few comments like 'That's really clever,

Susheela,' interspersed by thoughtful looks into the distance. He was actually racking his brains, thinking hard about how he could possibly avoid any part in the school's performing arts, and yet have his absence from the event go undetected. Inspiration proved elusive even as his furrowed brow conveyed the impression that he was listening to every word of Susheela's explanation.

Shortly after breakfast, Susheela was picked up for the skit rehearsal at school. Joyappa followed later, but drove slowly to the school campus, convinced that he would be bored to tears over the next few hours. After parking the car, he waited with the other parents outside the Great Hall, the venue for the day's activities. Most parents seemed excited to be there, and he could hear the mothers chattering and comparing notes about the roles their children were to play in the Variety Entertainment Programme.

He wandered aimlessly between the groups of people conversing about assorted subjects as they waited for the doors of the building to be opened. When he overheard some studious-looking people talking about research, publications, grants and other such matters, he hurriedly moved on. He had a suspicion that they were scientists and did not want to linger within earshot in the interests of his own sanity.

Joyappa also overheard many men discussing topics he neither knew nor cared about. One group talked about stocks and shares, Wall Street, Dalal Street and other matters that he assumed pertained to city life. He was somewhat perplexed when a tall man wearing horn-rimmed spectacles steered the conversation to bulls and bears. Joyappa concluded that the fellow was a city person who also owned a farm near the jungle.

Real estate, taxes, capital gains, cycling, calories, blood

pressure, creatinine levels or cholesterol; nothing, absolutely nothing, caught his interest.

Finally, he overheard a discussion about 'rum', 'bourbon' and 'beer', which almost caused him to trip over his feet as he changed direction and homed in on the source of these honeyed words. Joyappa found himself standing next to a couple of paunchy men, with slightly reddish complexions and eyes that heavy drinkers often develop. He listened with great interest as one of them admitted that he preferred Indian rum to anything from the Caribbean. Another argued that while some Indian brands were indeed superior, he preferred a certain Jamaican product for preparing cocktails.

Upon spotting Joyappa lurking in the vicinity, and instinctively identifying him as a kindred spirit, one of them said, 'Hi there, I'm Venky, and this is Sameer.' They were friendly and shook hands with Joyappa to welcome him into the group.

Venky was a tea planter from Valparai in Tamil Nadu. His hair was slicked down with a generous quantity of coconut oil. Sameer owned a resort in the high ranges of Kerala, and seemed to be hard of hearing, which explained why Venky had to speak loudly and often repeat himself.

'Hello, hello! Good to meet you,' said Joyappa, meaning every word. These men were not pretentious, their handshakes were firm and the topic of their discussion was right up Joyappa's alley. He joined the conversation and made meaningful contributions about his own alcoholic preferences.

Soon, the conversation veered to the upcoming entertainment programme. Venky's daughter was to participate in a classical dance recital, while Sameer's wife had been assigned a part in the parents' skit. Clearly, none of the three men wanted to sit though the long and potentially boring programme.

'Frankly, I would rather undergo a root canal than attend this event,' said Sameer.

'If I had an option, I would gladly walk over hot coals instead of being subjected to this sort of slow torture,' said Venky.

Not to be outdone, Joyappa said, 'Even though I hate the sensation, I would prefer to have my underwear infested with fleas.'

Despite Joyappa's bizarre statement, both Venky and Sameer nodded understandingly. This further endeared them to Joyappa.

'Well, why don't we do something about it?' said Venky. 'I've got some beer and rum stashed away in my car. When the programme begins, we could easily sneak out and spend a few hours in town. If we return before the finale, our wives and kids would be none the wiser about our having missed most of the boring performances.'

'Super idea, Venky,' said Sameer.

'I like the plan,' Joyappa responded, but with some trepidation. 'If my wife ever finds out, my life will be a living hell.'

'We could grab a bite at that nice Chinese restaurant in town,' Sameer suggested. 'I really look forward to eating there when I'm in Ooty. The food is always fresh and flavourful and never smothered in masala. I used to stuff myself so full that my wife no longer lets me eat there. Some rubbish about my lipid profiles being off the charts.'

'Let's do it,' agreed Joyappa, tossing caution to the winds, as the promise of liquor and a meal without restrictions proved too hard to resist.

'That's the spirit!' Venky said with a pleased look, before cleverly adding, 'All the better to enjoy *my* cache of spirits.'

As soon as the enormous Burma teak doors of the Great

Hall opened and the audience began to stream in, the three conspirators separated and sneaked off to the rendezvous at the parking lot. Sameer decided to drive as the windows of his vehicle were almost opaque, thanks to the tinted film—ultra-dark and illegal—he had installed. Venky extracted the liquor from the boot of his car, where it was concealed at the bottom of a plastic crate beneath filthy, grease-coated tools meant to deter his wife from prying.

The three men had the grace to wait until they had driven out of the school campus and parked by the side of an isolated potato field before they began to drink. After a few swigs, all of them concurred that the beer from a micro-brewery was tasty but lacked the kick offered by a certain cheap commercial brand. Much to the delight of his fellow drinkers, Venky then magically produced a few cans of their preferred beer.

The well-tended potato plants reminded Venky of a certain bottle of liquor amongst his other treasures. After imbibing some imported vodka, they decided it was time to hit the imaginatively named 'Noodles and Rice'. Located in Ooty, on top of a gentle hill, the restaurant was a favourite of generations of hungry students from the various boarding schools that dotted the hill station.

The procedure for ordering was efficient and prevented any miscommunication between customers and distracted waiters. Patrons were required to write the number corresponding to the dish listed on the menu on a paper 'chit' along with the desired quantity. By the time Joyappa and his fellow diners filled their order, most of the items on the menu had been listed.

The waiter had seen his share of hungry students but could not reconcile the quantity of food ordered and the number of guests. Somewhat puzzled, he asked Sameer, 'Sir, do you want some of these items packed?'

'No,' replied Sameer, emphatically.

'Sir, do you want the food parcelled, to take away?'

'Nope,' said Venky and Joyappa together.

'Will there be someone else joining you?' asked the waiter, persistently.

'Nyet,' replied Venky, whose vocabulary had expanded after the vodka.

The waiter shrugged but proceeded to do his job. He had to make multiple trips from the kitchen to the table, but his lumbago, varicose veins and fatigue were temporarily forgotten, as he observed with fascination the disappearance of vast amounts of soup and assorted dishes—lo mein, chowmein, hakka noodles, chilly chicken, chicken with cashew, sweet and sour pork, chop suey and various house specialities.

The men leaned back with their bellies pushing prominently against their waistbands, and into the edge of the table. They were satiated after their unsupervised feast but could not relax for long, as they needed to return to school before their absence was noted by their families.

Joyappa insisted on paying. It was, in his opinion, the very least he could do to thank his new friends for a wonderful day. When he thought no one was watching, he delved into the secret pocket of his underwear and extricated the 'slush fund' that he kept hidden from Susheela just for such contingencies.

After proclaiming that no meal was truly complete without dessert, Venky asked Sameer to stop at an iconic chocolate and pastry shop in the heart of the town. The famous chocolate éclairs from Modern Stores hit the spot and so did the Blue Mountain truffles.

Their haste to return to campus along the winding roads made the three new pals somewhat queasy. But they did manage to slip into the Great Hall during the final, climactic scene of the school play. The lead actor, who played a detective, had just accused a mild, wispy young woman of murder, and was explaining how he had reached this unlikely conclusion.

It was dark, so Joyappa thought he would slip into the nearest vacant seat near one of the exits. His recent excesses and hurried travel had left him feeling tired, and he sat down heavily with a sense of relief. The seat seemed surprisingly comfortable, and it was only when he leaned back that he heard a muffled 'Help! Save me!' from the well-upholstered woman he had inadvertently crushed.

Before Joyappa could react and lift his considerable bulk off the flailing victim, she had managed to grab a portion of his thigh and administered an excruciating pinch that caused him to squeal like a pig. As he desperately launched himself off the unfortunate woman, he could hear angry whispers asking him to 'shut up', 'leave the hall' and 'be considerate'. Joyappa crawled on all fours until he found a curtain near one of the rear exits and tried to hide behind it.

Despite the disturbance, the young performers—other than pausing briefly, which actually added to the tension—did a superb job of getting through the final scene. By the time the lights came on, Joyappa had composed himself, found a seat that was actually vacant and was applauding lustily like the rest of the audience. He was not able to spot Venky or Sameer but hoped they had managed to avoid getting into trouble. Although his inner thigh hurt terribly, he felt he had dodged a bullet.

When Joyappa met Susheela on the lawn after the show, he was effusive in his praise. 'You were superb, Susheela. Wow, wow, wow!'

'Oh, thanks Joy! That's sweet of you. Did you really think so?'

'Yup. You were excellent. The audience loved it.'

'Did I look like a model? Was the walk alright?'

'Well, in my opinion, those models should take lessons from you. They could learn a thing or two,' said Joyappa, hoping he hadn't laid it on too thick.

Susheela blushed and took his arm as she fished for more compliments, 'Aww, Joy. Are you sure?'

Several boys in blazers and ties suddenly appeared before them and wished them a good evening. Susheela was pleased to see her fellow long-distance runners.

'Hello, boys,' said Susheela, with a dazzling smile. 'Joy, these are the nice young men who were so helpful when I ran the cross-country race.'

'Good evening,' said Joyappa, but he was somewhat distracted. Following his faux pax during the play, he was afraid that someone might identify him, and was therefore anxious to leave the campus.

'Ma'am, we just wanted to tell you that you were superb in the skit,' said one of the bolder boys.

Susheela was thrilled and thanked the young man. Unfortunately, for her admirers, a master in charge of ensuring that students returned to their dormitories on time, rounded them up and sent them to their respective houses.

As Joyappa and Susheela strolled towards the parking lot, Susheela said, 'Wasn't Timmy great in the play? I thought he played the role of a nerdy scientist really well.'

Joyappa agreed enthusiastically. He had completely forgotten about Timmy and his play. He thought to himself that it would not have been much of a stretch for their son to play that role.

As they approached the parking lot, they could hear someone sobbing loudly. They looked around and found a plump, bejewelled woman in a black and gold sari, sniffing and dabbing her eyes as she spoke to a thin man in an expensive three-piece suit.

'I'm telling you, Raj. I am not imagining things. Some disgusting pervert rubbed himself all over me. It was horrible. You were absolutely of no help. You were actually snoozing.'

'But Deepa, I'm not sure such people would even be allowed into the Great Hall,' the thin man remarked helplessly, 'What would you like me to do?' he asked.

'I don't know Raj. Do something. Don't just stand there. Call the police. Don't you know a minister in Delhi? Call him. Do you believe this sort of thing should happen? At a school?'

'I promise to make enquiries tomorrow, Deepa. It has been a long day. Why don't we go back to the hotel and rest?' he suggested soothingly as he opened the door of a gleaming Mercedes supercar.

Deepa began to sob as she spoke to her husband, 'Let's pull our kids out of this place, Raj. I wish you hadn't donated that huge sum to the school for the new science building.'

She paused to wipe her eyes and said, 'He smelled of cheap liquor, and sweet and sour pork. It was just awful. I was afraid to scream as it would have disrupted the play. However, I did manage to pinch that dreadful fellow somewhere, and I thought he squealed.'

'Come on, Susheela,' said Joyappa quickly. 'We better get back to the bungalow. You must be tired after that great performance.'

'Okay, Joy,' Susheela replied as she curiously looked at the still upset Deepa and said, 'That poor woman. What kind of deviant takes advantage of a woman at a cultural show?'

'You are right. I wonder how on earth they get into places

like this. Terrible, isn't it?' concurred Joyappa, as he helped her into the car.

Susheela sniffed the air and said, 'That's odd. I can actually smell beer and sweet and sour pork, too.'

'You must be imagining things, Susheela,' said Joyappa, as he quickly rolled down the windows despite the evening chill. He resolved to shower and douse himself with cologne as soon as they returned to the bungalow.

To change the subject, Joyappa complimented Susheela by saying that she was a natural actor and suggesting that perhaps Timmy had inherited her talent. Susheela was pleased and squeezed his arm as she explained the creative message the director of the skit had wished to convey. Joyappa was relieved that her attention was diverted from Deepa. He pretended to listen as she prattled on.

While driving out of the parking lot, he overheard Deepa's additional instructions to her husband, 'When you lodge that complaint, in addition to being sweaty and smelly, be sure to say that he was a great big, hairy beast of a fellow. His arms rubbed against me and it seemed like they were covered in fur.'

2
Joy in School

The next morning, Joyappa and Susheela first attended the Arts and Crafts Show. There were numerous exhibits by the students and their teachers, including oil and watercolour paintings, besides sculptures in diverse materials and themes. Woodwork, needlework, handloom weaving and pottery products were the craft items on show. Several exhibits of varying quality were being offered for sale. Many of the parents bought the exhibits, usually focussing on their own children's products regardless of merit.

Although Susheela was quite interested in the show, nothing really caught Joyappa's fancy other than a piece of pottery in the shape of a beer tankard. The only item listed under Timmy's name was a sad-looking plaster of Paris sculpture of an animal. His parents craned their necks and viewed the exhibit from different angles but could not determine whether it was meant to be a parrot, an ostrich or a hippopotamus. Even Susheela, who was normally enthusiastic about anything pertaining to her son, couldn't bring herself to purchase the 'sculpture'.

Joyappa followed Susheela into the gleaming new science building somewhat reluctantly as he still retained unpleasant memories of the science classes he had to endure during his own school days. Groups of up to twenty visitors were provided a tour of the building wherein students gave short presentations about their projects through posters and practical demonstrations.

Predictably, Joyappa understood nothing and was quickly bored by the physics and chemistry displays. Susheela informed Joyappa that Timmy could have presented the findings from his chemistry experiments, but let his laboratory partner do so instead because his biology teacher had insisted that he prepare a poster on his botanical research.

Susheela was excited as they entered the hall where the biology presentations were being made. Joyappa thought he heard a little squeal of delight as they spotted Timmy.

Timmy's biology teacher was a young woman named Neena Berg. She was very attractive but seemed caught in a time warp. Her deportment and attire often resembled that of a Hollywood star from the 1950s. Rumour had it that some distant ancestor had travelled to India and fought as a mercenary for the army of a small princely state. He had fallen in love with a local woman, sired a large family and never returned to his European home.

Ms Berg was bright and seemed completely dedicated to teaching. Many younger, single males from the faculty had tried to be friendly with her, but she kept them all at a distance, prompting them to nickname her the 'Ice Berg' or 'Titanic'. Her departmental colleagues referred to her—with humour unique to botanists—as *Lactuca*, the Latin name for lettuce (of which iceberg is a common variety). Given her looks, and the hormonally charged teenagers on campus, it was only natural that many students were secretly enamoured of her. The only time she bestowed a smile upon anyone was when a student earned an 'A' in biology or obtained a particularly interesting result from an experiment.

Timmy stood by his poster, while Ms Berg stationed herself a few feet behind him. Normally, he carried himself diffidently, with a slightly stooped posture and numerous nervous twitches. His favourite mannerism, which irritated Joyappa immensely, was a slight wrinkling of his nose followed by a quick adjustment of his thick, horn-rimmed spectacles.

Timmy smiled when he saw his parents. He was fortunately professional enough not to hug his mother. Joyappa was pleased with Timmy's restraint and was relieved to see that the boy was standing upright, looking calm and, mercifully, not adjusting his glasses.

Timmy politely greeted the gathering of visitors and proceeded to explain the results of his school project. He told the group that he had isolated a 'putant' of a small plant called *Arabidopsis thaliana* that was popular as a 'model' for botanical experiments. When he stated that it belonged to the same family as Brussels sprouts, cabbage, broccoli and radishes, Joyappa gagged and fought the overwhelming urge to flee the building.

Timmy said, 'A putant is a putative mutant. This means the plant cannot be called an actual mutant until it is studied further. Interestingly, the plant seems to take a long time to age and remains green for much longer than a "normal" plant.' Timmy also speculated that changes in its hormonal levels delayed senescence and indicated that his findings could have long-term implications in the understanding and improvement of crop plants.

Timmy spoke clearly, concisely and with great confidence. Susheela felt overwhelmed and dabbed her eyes as she saw her 'tiny baby' conduct himself with such aplomb. Joyappa was very proud of the boy's scientific acumen, although he secretly wished that Timmy had also exhibited the same sort of aptitude for hockey.

Timmy concluded his presentation and answered all questions patiently and thoroughly. When the group began to move on to the next poster in the room, Timmy walked up to his parents.

Joyappa shook his hand and said, 'That was very interesting, Timmy. You did a fine job, son.'

'Thanks, Dad,' Timmy replied, positively glowing at the unexpected praise from his father.

Timmy indicated to his parents that he had to hurry back to his poster as the next batch of visitors had arrived. Joyappa continued to hold Susheela's arm in a firm grip as he was afraid, she would start hugging and kissing their son and ruin the young man's blazer with her tears.

Meanwhile, Ms Berg, who had hitherto observed Timmy's presentation with a satisfied look, approached Joyappa and Susheela, and introduced herself. Her hair was pulled back into a severe bun; yet, she was clearly an attractive woman.

'You should be very proud of Timmy,' she said, warmly. 'I believe he has a bright future as he demonstrates great aptitude for science and is well ahead of his contemporaries. You must have seen his excellent poster in the Department of Chemistry presented by his lab partner. Although I helped him with this project, he did come up with some very interesting insights on his own. I sincerely hope you encourage him to pursue a career in science.'

Ms Berg's praise led to Susheela's flow of tears to resemble the mighty River Cauvery during peak monsoon. So, it was left to Joyappa to thank the young woman for her kind words and guidance. Ms Berg seemed concerned about Susheela and patted her on the back. Susheela continued to sob as she made her way outside, where she hoped to regain her composure.

Ms Berg whispered to Joyappa, 'Is she alright? Is she depressed?'

'No, no. But if she keeps this up, she might become dehydrated,' replied Joyappa quite seriously.

Ms Berg, who clearly appeared to be impressed by Joyappa, threw back her head and laughed a lovely, trilling sound that few on the campus had ever heard before. Then, she said, 'Oh, you are so clever. I know from where Timmy got his brains.'

Whether Ms Berg was just impressed to meet the father of one of her best students, or was overwhelmed by Joyappa's rugged outdoorsy looks, was not clear. Regardless, the woman's response was quite out of character, and would have turned her many admirers green with envy.

Joyappa reflected that if he had had a teacher like Neena Berg in school instead of the grumpy old man who had caned his tender behind every other day, he might well have pursued a career in science and even earned a PhD. Joyappa's logic completely overlooked the fact that when he was a teenager (and already sporting a remarkably thick moustache), a chemistry teacher had pleaded with his parents to enrol him in kindergarten once again. He also conveniently forgot about the bright young physics teacher who, shortly after evaluating Joyappa's exam paper, quit the noble profession. Joyappa thanked Ms Berg once more and moved away to join Susheela outside the building.

Susheela's emotional outburst was brought on by seeing Timmy presenting his work with such confidence. She felt pride but also a sense of loss that her little baby was growing up and had become more independent. She worried that he wouldn't need his 'Mummykins' anymore. She was concerned that he might go to a distant college, and later take up a job halfway across the world, and she would be only able to see him once every decade or so.

Joyappa's shortcomings in the field of science were numerous, but he was even more inept at comforting a crying woman. Despite the best of intentions, he had somehow mastered the ability to make things much worse.

Joyappa tried to calm Susheela by patting her on the back. But he patted too hard, and actually caused her to whimper in pain. Then, he told her that as soon as Timmy was done with school, he would like to send him abroad to get the best education possible, perhaps in London, or even Tel Aviv.

Susheela shoved her entire handkerchief into her mouth to keep from screaming. If she could have laid her hands on an *odikatti*, the fearsome knife traditionally used by her ancestors for close combat, there's no telling which part of Joyappa's anatomy would have been severed.

Susheela did the next best thing and made her way to the ladies' room to avoid any further words of 'comfort'. Joyappa felt proud of his abilities to soothe distraught women as he watched her stagger away between the many parents drinking tea on the lawn. He was sure she would feel much better after reflecting upon his words of wisdom.

Joyappa dismissed all thoughts of Susheela's discomfiture as soon as he spotted Venky and Sameer standing in the shade of a magnolia tree. His new pals greeted him effusively as kindred spirits are hard to come by in one's middle age. Sameer grumbled about being forced to play for the Parents' Cricket XI. Joyappa also expressed his reservations about participating in the match against the school team.

Venky, however, surprised them by saying, 'Fellows, I've been asked to captain the Parents' XI. You do not know this, but I was the captain of my university team and actually played a bit of first-class cricket in my youth.'

'Good for you, but I don't want to stand in the sun for hours, or get hit by a ball, Venky,' Sameer said, doubtfully.

'I played a lot of hockey in college, Venky. But I'm awful at cricket,' Joyappa added.

'Don't worry, Sameer. You can be the twelfth man and serve us refreshments during the drinks breaks. And Joy, I can have you stationed where no one is likely to hit a ball, so you won't have to run around or dive when we are fielding.'

'That could work', said Sameer, sounding quite relieved.

'Please turn up for the match or the School XI will be awarded a walkover. Also, just imagine how I will feel if you aren't there and I have to deal with the other parents by myself,' Venky added, as the three friends paused to listen to the ebb and flow of conversation from other areas of the lawn. They overheard discussions on boring subjects including triglycerides, ulcers, NASDAQ, futures, real estate and shopping in exotic locales.

Joyappa felt a wave of sympathy as he said, 'Fine, Venky, I'll be there. But don't put me in an awkward position during the match.'

'Don't you worry, pal,' Venky said confidently, 'Everything will be fine. Just make sure you are in spotless whites, so you actually look like a cricketer,' he added.

Venky was pleased. Before there could be any further discussion, Joyappa saw Susheela forlornly sipping tea in the distance. So, he wished his friends goodbye and made his way towards her. He knew from his experience as a hockey player that dehydration could be a very serious condition. He hoped the tea would replace the fluids she had lost while crying.

Joyappa awoke to the hooting of a Nilgiri langur. Susheela refused to leave the bed, as she was still feeling distraught (or 'dehydrated', in Joyappa's opinion) after the exhibition.

Joyappa took the opportunity to devour a dozen fluffy idlis with sambar, and several crisp wadas smothered in spicy tomato chutney. Abraham was as efficient as ever in providing him with a couple of pots of freshly brewed filter coffee.

Susheela still hadn't surfaced when Joyappa coolly slipped on his almost opaque sunglasses and left the bungalow. He hoped the day's cricket would not be too demanding. Driving through Ooty, he suddenly remembered that Venky had insisted that the team be attired in proper white cricketing gear. As he was running a little late for the match, he stopped at a sports goods shop, and hurriedly picked up a white jersey and pants.

A short distance out of town, Joyappa realized that he was wearing his bright orange underwear with neon green polka dots. He thought they were incredibly comfortable, and even added a classy touch to his appearance. However, as Venky had instructed that he needed to 'look like a cricketer', he didn't want to upset the captain by having flashes of colour peeking through when he stretched or bent during the course of the game.

So, Joyappa made an abrupt U-turn, and almost collided with the shiny new Mercedes that was closely following him. The driver braked abruptly causing the car to nearly skid off the road. Joyappa saw the driver shaking his fist angrily at him and thought he might have heard the faint sound of a woman's scream. However, Joyappa was too focussed on his important mission to be side-tracked by such trivial issues. He drove through town with reckless abandon, parked illegally and charged into the nearest shop. He was relieved to spot on a shelf nearby, a dark coloured package—although everything seemed dark through his sunglasses—that appeared to have a picture of underwear on the front.

'Are those white?' he asked the teenaged salesgirl with some urgency.

'Yes, sir,' she replied tentatively. 'We also have an offer on it. 'You get six for the price of five, and we have them in double XL too,' she added.

'Gimme,' said Joyappa brusquely. Noticing that the girl looked scared, he remembered to smile before adding, 'No need to pack it. Thanks.'

He tossed some money on the counter, grabbed the package and asked the girl to keep the change. Relieved to see his car hadn't been towed, Joyappa jumped in, made an illegal U-turn and sped off to the cricket ground at the Cold Mountain Academy.

Joyappa found his way to the visitors' dressing room. He was the last one to arrive as almost everyone else was already dressed in their white uniforms. Some of the men were stretching, while a few others were talking to a skinny man, who was visibly upset.

'Cheer up, Raj,' said a portly fellow wearing glasses. 'At least you came through unscathed.'

Raj, who Joyappa remembered seeing in the parking lot after the school play, angrily replied, 'I wish I'd got the blighter's number. It was a touch and go, and I barely managed to avoid driving off the cliff. Poor Deepa was so scared, she screamed.'

Raj paused to take a sip of Alpine spring water. He swallowed, causing his prominent Adam's apple to wobble erratically, before continuing with his story, 'It happened so quickly that I am not even sure what colour the car was. All I could see was a crude, chunky-looking fellow with really dark glasses. This sort of scum should have their licenses revoked and be restricted to driving bullock carts.'

Joyappa instantly removed his sunglasses and slipped them into his bag in one swift motion. He turned his back to Raj, hoping he wouldn't be recognized.

Others made sympathetic noises and agreed with Raj. They were all of the opinion that drivers who took abrupt and illegal U-turns should be banned.

The portly fellow removed his glasses, and polishing them with a silk handkerchief, he said, 'You know the local people in the Nilgiris are so polite. They are such considerate drivers that it must have been one of those uncouth tourists from the plains.'

Joyappa was happy to see Venky, who said, 'Glad you made it, Joy. Take the locker next to Sameer's. After you've changed, join us on the ground for a warm-up session before the match.'

Sameer greeted Joyappa warmly and said, 'I'm glad I'm not playing, Joy. Venky wants me to carry the drinks out to the field during breaks. Don't look so worried, buddy. I'll make sure you are in good spirits.'

The men trooped out leaving Joyappa with Sameer. Raj, still looking upset, was at the far end of the room. Raj placed his Gucci loafers in the locker and began to change into his spotless white Tommy Hilfiger jersey and pants.

Joyappa tore open the package that he had hurriedly purchased in Ooty. He was glad to see that the new undergarments were, in fact, white. However, as they seemed a bit bulky, he decided to keep wearing his lucky orange and green briefs and pulled on the new 'underwear' over them.

Sameer stood up and stared, 'Hey, Joy. That's really brilliant. I wish I had thought of wearing adult diapers myself. A few beers, and the old bladder starts to rebel, if you know what I mean. I've got to start doing that. Super idea, man.'

Adult diapers! Joyappa was surprised. He had no clue about the true function of his 'underwear' until Sameer's statement. Yet, he wasn't one to turn down a compliment.

'Thanks, Sameer,' said Joyappa modestly. Then, he offered Sameer three diapers from the half dozen he had purchased and said, 'Better safe than sorry, huh?'

Neither Joyappa nor Sameer noticed that Raj, who had dabbed on some expensive French cologne, was staring at Joyappa with an extremely horrified look. A childhood memory of a popular cartoon character, Baby Huey, fleetingly crossed his mind. This memory was quickly erased upon closer inspection of the hirsute figure before him.

As he stared at the diaper, Raj couldn't help but notice the discoloured, bruised area on Joyappa's thick inner thigh. Fortunately, for Joyappa, Raj didn't realize that it was an outcome of Deepa's attempt to defend herself during the school play. Raj speculated that the awful, paunchy, hairy fellow's diaper must have given way and caused that horrible rash.

Raj shuddered. He was not sure if it was even safe to share a locker room with this man-child wearing adult diapers. He quickly doused himself with even more cologne, smeared generous amounts of hand sanitizer onto every exposed inch of his body and scurried out of the room.

Venky and the captain of the school team, Coach Dorai, walked out to the cricket field for the toss. Venky won and chose to field. True to his promise, Venky had Joyappa fielding at 'long leg', close to the boundary rope where a large tree provided welcome shade. The ball rarely came his way and when it did, he was able to pick it up and return it to the wicket keeper with minimal effort. Soon, he was beset with ennui. He observed that there was no turf where he was fielding, so he picked up a twig and began to play 'Noughts and Crosses' in the mud by himself.

The School XI coasted along, and seemed set for a large score, until Venky brought himself on to bowl. Using his wiles and experience, he was able to fox the batsmen with sharp leg spin and googlies, and wickets began to fall at regular intervals. Eventually, the School XI fought back and was able to string together a partnership between Coach Dorai and Kumar, one of the most promising young players in the school's long history.

The sun began to beat down intensely and many of Joyappa's teammates, used to working in air-conditioned offices, began to struggle with the heat. Sameer brought out drinks at regular intervals, which most of the fielders accepted gratefully. Raj, however, refused to drink the lemonade and would trot off the field where his wife Deepa in a pink designer outfit, dispensed premium Alpine spring water from a cooler.

Sameer invariably served Joyappa last, accompanied by a subtle wink. After the second drinks interval, Joyappa experienced a pleasant buzz as his lemonade had been supplemented with generous amounts of gin.

He was grateful to Sameer, as he was starting to feel bored with his solitary game. He found that victory was assured regardless of whether he started with a 'nought' or a 'cross', and the predictable wins were making him restless. So, he started doodling on the ground. He first drew a bottle of beer. Unsatisfied with the result, he began to vigorously kick some earth over his 'artwork'.

Meanwhile, Coach Dorai, one of the few people capable

of negotiating Venky's bowling, hit the ball powerfully towards the boundary. Joyappa was blissfully unaware that the ball was racing towards him. Luckily for the team, Joyappa's foot—in the process of erasing the clumsily-drawn beer bottle—accidentally made contact with the ball. The unexpected impact caused a sharp pain in his foot.

'Nice stop, Joy,' Venky shouted, pleased that a boundary had been saved.

'Ow, ow, ow!' Joyappa howled in agony. He was on the verge of swearing, when he realized he was on a school campus, and his favourite curse words must not fall upon tender ears. Instead, he directed his fury at the ball and, using his thick powerful legs, kicked it hard. Cricket balls tend to be firm and unforgiving, and, in his anger, Joyappa instinctively and foolishly kicked the ball with his injured foot. He screamed in anguish. The ball travelled across the field like a tracer bullet and, quite improbably, knocked over one of the wickets.

Coach Dorai was stranded out of his crease. He was clearly out. It left him stunned. He had never been dismissed in such a bizarre manner in his long and distinguished cricketing career. Joyappa's teammates were ecstatic, but most of them were feeling too hot and tired to run down to congratulate him. The large number of students and other supporters of the School XI were stunned into silence at Coach Dorai's strange dismissal. Meanwhile, Joyappa remained oblivious to his heroic deed. The pain in his foot had abated sufficiently for him to resume his artistic endeavours in the soil, where he attempted to draw a beer mug topped with foam.

Ms Berg, who had just concluded a discussion with her colleague pertaining to the latest theory on the mode of action of gibberellins, had observed the whole incident. She was highly impressed.

'That is the father of my best student,' she told her colleague. 'He's so charming and rugged.'

'Oh, really!' said the colleague, sarcastically. He was a young man who harboured a secret crush on her.

'What a way to get someone out! He's so clever, to boot,' Ms Berg added, before laughing at her inadvertent pun.

The young man was stunned. He had never heard 'Ice Berg' laugh. He felt crushed, and soon assumed the appearance of a whipped puppy.

On the field, Kumar, the young star of the school team was proving to be a thorn in the flesh of the Parents' XI. A few more wickets had fallen; yet, despite Venky's guile and prowess, Kumar continued to score freely as he farmed the strike and shielded the last batsman.

Joyappa was negotiating a different sort of problem. A couple of flies, possibly attracted by his alcohol-flavoured sweat, were bothering him. He flapped his hands about, but they wouldn't go away. So, he decided to stay still and pretend that he was unaware of their presence. His plan was to swat them when they least expected it. Eventually one of the flies landed on his shoulder, but Joyappa waited patiently until it crawled onto his left cheek. When it paused to do whatever flies do upon pausing, Joyappa unleashed a powerful open-handed blow designed to kill it. The fly, however, took flight a nanosecond before Joyappa's palm landed. Joyappa swore under his breath as he felt the sting of the blow. Like any good hunter, he decided that his plan required revision. For his second attempt, Joyappa resolved to smash the pesky insects while they were still in the air, much like a tennis player countering a lob at Wimbledon.

At this juncture, the 'glorious uncertainty' of cricket manifested itself. Kumar hooked a short ball from Raj. The powerfully struck ball hurtled towards the boundary for what appeared to be a definite 'six'. At the same moment, Joyappa leapt up to carry out an overhead smash on a particularly pesky fly. Before he could execute the plan—and indeed the fly—the ball collided with his open hand.

Joyappa screamed in pain but was so shocked to find the unexpected object in his palm that he forgot to swear. Miraculously, the ball 'stuck' to Joyappa's hand, and a stunned Kumar was forced to head back to the pavilion. Joyappa was annoyed that the fly had escaped and threw the ball back to the bowler with a disgusted look. Then, he heard applause and realized he had done something significant.

The catch was spectacular as the ball, travelling at great velocity, seemed destined to cross the boundary. Joyappa's leap had been accidental but timed so perfectly that any professional player would have been proud to take such a catch. Joyappa's teammates soon clustered around him, patted him on the back and high-fived his sore palm.

Even Raj, who got credit for the wicket, smiled weakly from a safe distance and murmured, 'Jolly good catch', but made no attempt to shake hands or make contact with any part of Joyappa's anatomy.

Venky, the captain, was showering compliments and exclaimed, 'Wow! What a dramatic end to their innings! That was a fantastic catch, Joy. If I had known you were such a superb fielder, I would have had you patrolling the covers.'

'What can I say, Venky? We all have our hidden talents,' replied Joyappa, with a self-effacing smile.

Unlike the rest of their team mates, who were in the pavilion, Joyappa and Sameer decided to relax outdoors until Joyappa was required to don his batting gear. They were reclining in the shade of a large shrub on a grassy bank with a good view of the ground as they both sipped some 'fortified' lemonade. In keeping with his duties as twelfth man, Sameer had also produced an ice pack from somewhere for Joyappa's sore palm. Soon both of them dozed off.

Venky and Raj strolled out to open the innings for the Parents' XI. Raj, who had once played for his university, was to take strike and asked the umpire for middle-stump guard.

Kumar, the opening bowler of the School XI, stretched his muscular body. His run up began so far away that Raj started to feel nervous as the young man charged towards the crease. The first ball sailed past the off stump before Raj could even lift his bat. Raj was petrified as he had never faced a bowler of such express pace. Raj didn't even see the second ball as it whistled past his nose. The third ball missed his off stump by a whisker, while the fourth almost kissed the bails. When Kumar started to bowl the fifth ball, Raj was so terrified that he wished he could have borrowed a diaper from Joyappa. As the ball thudded into his rib cage, he let out an inadvertent squeak. He just wanted to flee and hide. However, Deepa was watching and he didn't want her to believe he was a coward. The final ball of Kumar's over was a fast in-swinger that pitched on a good length and cannoned into Raj's stomach. Poor Raj collapsed on the stumps in an ungainly heap. He was out hit wicket and the Parents XI lost their first batsman for no score.

A woman's high-pitched wail awakened Joyappa from his nap. Turning towards the source, he saw Deepa blubbering over Raj, who was doubled over and moaning as he clutched his stomach just outside the pavilion.

'Oh, Sweetums, what happened?'

'Owwww,' Raj exclaimed.

'Why have we had such miserable luck this week? I just don't understand. First, I get assaulted while watching the school play by a "sweet and sour pork-eating" pervert.'

'Aaaaaah,' said poor Raj, who was tired of hearing about the alleged assault and would have liked an ice pack on his painful abdomen, instead of having to hear Deepa recounting the incident again. Unmindful of his agony, Deepa continued to whine.

'Then, today some insane man almost runs us off a mountain. We could have been *killed*, Raj.'

'Some ice, pleeease!' Raj whimpered.

'You know how much that Mercedes cost, Raj. Daddy bought it for me on my birthday. It is a beauty. Top of the line, with all the bells and whistles. Can you imagine how I would have felt if my present had been ruined by that dreadful driver with those terribly dark, cheap sunglasses?'

Joyappa was quite offended by the rude reference to his glasses. He had to exercise iron self-discipline to refrain from correcting Deepa and giving himself away. They were his favourite shades and had set him back a small fortune. *How dare she criticize them*, he thought.

'Owwwwww. Need an ice pack,' Raj mumbled weakly.

'I wish you would stop mewling when I am talking about important things, Raj. You *never* pay any attention to me. Daddy *always* listens to me and helps me,' Deepa remarked as she began to cry.

Raj decided to take matters into his own hands and walked painfully into the pavilion where they had left their cooler. Deepa followed him, still complaining about her traumatic experience while demonstrating little sympathy for the injured man. When

Raj opened the container, he was shocked. There was no ice pack!

'Deepa,' he croaked. 'Where's the ice pack? I can't find it.'

'I want to see Daddy. Please Raj, drive me home, where people are civilized. At least, the perverts in our city have better personal hygiene,' said Deepa through her tears.

This was too much for Raj, who staggered outside, looked to the heavens and summoned up enough energy to scream, 'Aaaaaahhhhhh! Help! I need my ice pack. Pleeeeease!'

The loud scream shocked everyone nearby and even interrupted Sameer's slumber. He sat up. One look was enough for him to assess the situation and accurately determine what exactly had upset Raj. He swiftly yanked the ice pack from Joyappa's hand and threw it into some shrubs, thereby removing all evidence of his clandestine raid of Raj's cooler.

During this off-field drama, the School XI, led by Kumar's fearsome pace bowling and Coach Dorai's astute off spin, had dismissed several parents. Standing tall amongst the ruins was Venky, who was masterfully accumulating runs while shielding less competent batsmen from the school team's potent bowling attack.

With more than half the batting side dismissed, Joyappa was summoned to the pavilion. He put on his protective gear and promptly nodded off once again. When the penultimate wicket fell, it was Joyappa's turn to bat. However, he remained oblivious to the action on the field and the state of the game. Next to him, Sameer too, snored gently.

Someone prodded Joyappa and said, 'You're up! It's your turn to bat.'

Joyappa stood up, stretched and headed to the crease. His approach was similar in some respects to that of the legendary West Indian, Sir Isaac Vivian Alexander Richards. 'Viv' Richards was arguably the most dominant batsman of his era, who refused to wear a helmet while he played some of the fastest bowlers in the world. Viv's confident swagger, quicksilver reflexes, fearlessness and obvious talent were enough to intimidate the opposition.

Joyappa, too, wore no helmet as he staggered towards the centre of the ground. He too was courageous and blessed with the fearless heart of a warrior—even if the heart had to endure levels of lipids and alcohol that most hearts never encounter in a lifetime. However, watching his zig-zag approach to the crease elicited sniggers from the fielding team and filled them with confidence.

Venky, the non-striker, walked up to Joyappa and said, 'Joy, just block the ball and give me the strike. We need just fifteen runs to win.'

'Sure, Venky,' said Joyappa confidently. He was breathing heavily and Venky recoiled at the overpowering odour of gin.

Venky was worried. He had brought the Parents' XI to the cusp of victory, but he hadn't counted on having to win the game with a drunk, uncoordinated partner.

Kumar smiled confidently as he assured his captain, 'Skipper, I'll get this joker out in no time. The game is as good as won.'

The chirpy wicket keeper of the School XI decided to scare Joyappa for good measure. He taunted, 'Hey, Paunchy! Just stay out of the way and get out bowled; that way, we won't have to carry you off on a stretcher.' Undaunted, Joyappa assumed his stance.

Kumar bowled a fine outswinger that may have got a top order batsman out. Joyappa neither saw the ball nor moved, so there was no danger of his nicking it and getting dismissed. The next ball was a bouncer that whistled past his face, ruffling his moustache in the process. The third ball thudded into Joyappa's bat before he could move and, to Venky's relief, they managed to take a run that got Joyappa off strike. Venky negotiated the rest of Kumar's over safely and scored a run off the last ball.

In the next over, Venky scored 10 runs off Coach Dorai's tricky spin bowling. But, despite his best efforts, he could not retain strike for the last over of the match. This meant that Kumar would bowl the final over, and Joyappa would have to face him again.

Venky was tense as he said, 'Joy, you've got to somehow try to get a single. No matter what you do, don't get out. And, by the way, shall I ask Sameer to get you a helmet?'

'Not a prob, Venks,' said Joyappa, unconcerned. 'If I can't get a single off the first two balls, let's just run after the third ball is bowled.'

'Okay, I guess,' said Venky, doubtfully.

Kumar's first ball pitched and deviated sharply inwards. Joyappa leapt up and the evasive action prevented serious injury to his groin. However, the ball painfully scraped his prominent behind on its way to the wicket keeper. It hurt, but Joyappa's expression remained inscrutable. He refused to rub his posterior, as he did not want to grant his opponents the satisfaction of witnessing his suffering.

Kumar, an admirer of the Australian art of 'sledging', said, 'Hey, Chubbs! What do you eat to get a rear end like that?'

Joyappa seriously considered telling him that *pandi curry* swimming in fat, chased down with beer, would give anyone a prominent rear end. But when he saw Kumar smirking and the wicket keeper sniggering, he realized that it was not a polite question that required a courteous answer. Instead, he glared at Kumar and said, 'Shut up and bowl, kid.'

Kumar's second ball was a slower delivery. Instead of

attempting to get a single, Joyappa swung his bat wildly. He was unable to make contact with the ball and, fortunately for him, it narrowly missed his off stump.

Venky threw his hands in the air and shouted, 'Watch the ball, Joy. Don't do anything foolish.'

Thanks to the gin so thoughtfully provided by Sameer, Joyappa had been seeing three balls coming at him while he was batting. He wasn't sure which one he must try to hit. He had played the one on the left and missed. The outcome was the same when he tried to hit the ball on the right. So, Joyappa decided to play the one in the middle.

The sledging continued. The wicketkeeper yelled out to the bowler, 'Kumar, avoid that huge rear end and aim for the stumps. I bet a rump roast made from this clown would feed the whole school for a week.'

Kumar actually threw his head back and laughed. 'Yup. Throw in a couple of those thick thighs and you could feed the whole district!'

Joyappa was furious. Anger somehow cleared the alcohol-induced fog, and he became more alert. Now all he wanted was to teach Kumar and that annoying wicketkeeper a lesson. The sensible strategy discussed with Venky was completely forgotten.

Kumar's next delivery was a fast, good length ball aimed at the middle stump. Instead of playing a defensive shot, Joyappa took a mighty, unorthodox heave at the middle of the three balls that he saw racing towards him. Fortunately for him, the ball met the 'sweet spot' of the bat with a loud and satisfying *crack*! Joyappa held his pose as he watched the ball disappear. Fuelled by his anger, the powerfully struck ball soared into the air and crossed the midwicket boundary for a six! The Parents had won!

Venky, thrilled at the completely unexpected turn of events, charged down the pitch. He jumped on Joyappa, causing the hero to fall in a heap.

Kumar clutched his head in despair. The players of School XI were shattered; they just couldn't believe that the apparently inebriated, incompetent last batsman had beaten them when victory was within their grasp.

Joyappa's jubilant teammates left the pavilion and charged onto the field. The parents were clearly thrilled to have 'bragging rights' as none of them wanted to lose to the staff and students. Except for Raj who maintained a safe distance, they made a valiant effort to hoist Joyappa on their shoulders but failed miserably. After all, affluent stockbrokers, titans of industry and other white-collar professionals weren't exactly accustomed to heavy lifting. So, they restricted themselves to congratulating the hero by vigorously patting him on the back.

Joyappa basked in the adulation. Despite his reservations about playing, things couldn't have turned out better.

Amidst these scenes of jubilation and despair, no one was concerned about the fate of the cricket ball. Once it had crossed the boundary, the ball ricocheted off a eucalyptus tree that overlooked the visitors' parking lot. The tree, damaged during the previous monsoon, had one of its branches attached to the trunk by just a few fibres. Unfortunately, the gardeners, in their anxiety to ensure that the annuals bloomed at the right time, had not noticed its precarious state.

It is debatable whether it was mere coincidence, or if it was the cricket ball that caused the branch to separate from the tree. Whatever the reason, shortly after Joyappa's heroics, the branch hurtled downwards and landed with a loud crash upon Deepa's prized Mercedes. The ball then bounced on the tarred surface of the parking lot and rolled away harmlessly into the nearby shrubbery.

After a good night's rest, Susheela was feeling much better, but not quite normal. A few months previously, her friend Asha had returned from an excursion to eastern Europe with bottles of red pills that she referred to as 'mother's little helpers'. Susheela was usually disinclined to take any medication of dubious origin; however, she had been feeling so miserable at the thought of Timmy growing up and possibly moving to another country that she decided mother needed a little 'help'. Susheela had thus extricated the pills from a secret compartment in her handbag and swallowed a couple.

Miraculously, almost all her sad feelings were wiped away within a short time. She felt alive, her senses were heightened and she felt ready to face the world. Joyappa, although unaware of the reason for Susheela's improved mood, was pleased that she wasn't in that weepy, depressed state that he disliked almost as much as her fault-finding missions.

On campus, Joyappa and Susheela took their seats at the edge of a large field to observe the traditional military-style parade that had remained essentially unaltered for over a century. The students had been coached by a retired army drill instructor for months and were expected to carry out a flawless performance. The students' dark blue woollen uniforms were spotless, with brass buttons and badges polished to a high sheen. Their black leather shoes encased in sparkling white *puttees*—cloth that was spirally wrapped around their lower legs—added to the spectacle as they marched onto the ground.

Joyappa noticed that Susheela's skin was rather warm to the touch, she smiled frequently and there was an odd glint in her eyes. He asked if she had a fever, but she brushed off his concern and assured him that she was just fine.

Joyappa spotted Timmy in the Brass Band. Joyappa knew that his son played some obscure curved instrument, but he could never remember its name. Timmy had turned out as well as the other students, but was frequently out of step, and often had to perform a quick little skip to get back in sync. Rather than mention Timmy's ineptitude to Susheela, Joyappa wisely kept his counsel.

Susheela however, mistakenly identified a bespectacled trumpet player in the band as their son and excitedly pointed him out to Joyappa. As this young man *was* actually able to march in step, Joyappa did not bring up her error.

There was not a single cloud visible in the sky and the sun scorched the parade ground. The students patiently awaited the chief guest's arrival. A couple of younger boys fainted and were carried away for medical treatment. The next casualty was a tall girl, who was fortunately led off the ground before she collapsed. While Susheela was rummaging through her bag for her camera, Joyappa saw Timmy fall forward. His large brass instrument perhaps saved him from landing face first onto the ground and possibly breaking his thick glasses and injuring his nose. Joyappa was concerned but felt reassured when the boy was quickly taken away by the attentive medical staff. Fearful that Susheela might charge across the parade ground and embarrass everyone by administering CPR to Timmy, Joyappa made no mention of their son's premature exit.

The chief guest, an Air Marshal, who was a former test pilot in the Indian Air Force and veteran of many daring battles, arrived at the assigned time. When Joyappa saw the title 'Air Marshal' listed in the programme, he had expected a master of *martial* arts in the mould of his celluloid heroes, Chuck Norris and Bruce Lee. So, he was a little disappointed to observe a distinguished looking older man with a slight paunch.

The parade went off without a hitch. Susheela took innumerable pictures with the nervous energy and quivering hands caused by her exotic pills. Many of the photographs were of the bespectacled boy she thought was Timmy. Predictably, they were all badly out of focus. She also inadvertently captured several images of the sky, the treetops and the well-polished shoes of the marching students.

After the parade, the parents, alumni and senior students assembled in a large auditorium, where the headmaster addressed the audience. He spoke extensively about the many accomplishments of those associated with the school during the previous academic year. He highlighted the achievements of the students and lauded the efforts of the dedicated teaching faculty and support staff. The speech also explained his vision for the future of the grand old school and concluded in a far from subtle pitch for donations from the well-heeled audience.

Joyappa dozed off through most of the proceedings as the auditorium was comfortably warm, and he was somewhat sore and tired from his exertions on the cricket field the previous day. Susheela's hands, still quivering from the dubious medication, photographed the backs of the heads of people sitting in front of them, the ceiling of the auditorium, a prominent mole on the cheek of a chemistry teacher and the chief guest's left ear.

The venerable Air Marshal's speech was directed at the students who were about to enter the 'real world'. He urged these youngsters to consider enlisting in the armed forces as a means to serve the country, acquire various skills and travel the world. He advised them to live their lives with honour by shunning the corrupt practices that threatened to rock the foundations of our great nation. He went on to highlight his own heroic acts in numerous dogfights over the 'Western Front', destruction of enemy munitions dumps in the 'Eastern Theatre', clandestine reconnaissance trips 'up north' and 'down south' and the daring rescue of 'our boys' from behind enemy lines. The students were enthralled, and many of them resolved to serve the country by joining the armed forces.

He concluded by thundering, 'When you leave these hallowed halls of learning, remember that you must be leaders. Be great leaders of men, not mere sheep or 'yes-men'. Go forth into the world with confidence. Good luck to you all!'

The stirring speech was met with applause. The applause would have been even more resounding if the 'old school' Air Marshal had not excluded a significant portion of the audience in his final remarks. The women and girls in the auditorium were unhappy that the Chief Guest had made no mention of people of the female persuasion in his rousing conclusion.

As the applause died down, one bright and bold girl, in a startling break from protocol—which prescribed that chief guests were not to be interrupted or questioned—stood up. Even as her class teacher desperately tried to shush her, she asked in a clear, piping voice, 'But Sir, what about women?'

The chief guest realized his error and responded accordingly. 'Oh! Absolutely, my dear! I must apologize to all of you for the oversight. I certainly did not mean to exclude *anyone*. I am afraid I happened to use an archaic figure of speech. We do need fine young women participating in all walks of life.

Indeed, I am hopeful that the girls from this august institution will lead our nation to greater glory.'

The second round of applause was deafening. The chief guest took his seat with a broad smile on his face.

While lunch was being served on the school lawns, Joyappa visited the infirmary to check on Timmy. The school nurse informed him that the medical staff had administered first aid to everyone who had fainted during the parade. They were kept under observation to ensure no lasting damage had occurred. Further, as all the students had recovered completely, they had been sent back to their respective dormitories.

Joyappa was relieved. He returned to the school lawns in search of lunch (and Susheela). He was shocked to find his wife engaged in an intense conversation with Deepa. Joyappa quickly hid behind a tree and saw Deepa sobbing. Susheela put an arm around her in an effort to comfort the distraught woman. Raj was standing next to them, and although he wasn't weeping copiously, Joyappa saw him wipe his eyes with a silk handkerchief several times.

Joyappa was terrified that he had been recognized as the perpetrator of misdeeds against the couple and was worried that they might be complaining to Susheela about him. He briefly considered leaving. Then he saw that the lunch looked interesting. So, he grabbed a plate and piled it high with sandwiches and crisps. Susheela continued to listen to Deepa while holding her close. Joyappa's curiosity got the better of him, so he sidled over to a nearby shrub, turned his back to them and tried to eavesdrop on the conversation.

'Oh, you poor things,' Susheela was saying.

'I think the underworld is trying to get us,' said Deepa with a loud sob. 'Can you imagine being smothered by a smelly beast while enjoying a play? And, and...'

'There, there' Susheela said comfortingly as a fresh stream of tears ran down Deepa's cheeks. 'What kind of person would try to kill us by running us off the road? I just got a brief glimpse of him, but he looked evil, with a big moustache and dark glasses. I hear mobsters wear dark sunglasses, so their victims can't see their eyes or their expressions. Do you think the mob is sending us a message?' Deepa continued.

'I don't know dear, but couldn't it have been an accident?' Susheela questioned logically.

Joyappa quickly slipped off his sunglasses. He then heard an odd sound and turned his head slightly. Using his peripheral vision, he saw Raj's skinny legs making a strange movement that caused his knees to knock against one another.

Deepa ignored Susheela's call to reason and continued, 'On top of all that, poor Raj was hit in the stomach while playing cricket. You don't think the Cosa Nostra has infiltrated the school and tried to maim him, do you?'

'Unlikely, dear,' Susheela responded soothingly.

'You are so kind,' Deepa said gratefully. She then sighed, took a deep breath and continued in a low voice, 'When Raj's stomach was hurt, those bad, bad men even stole our ice pack. The goons then broke the windscreen of my beautiful, new Mercedes. Oh, I wish my daddy was here, he would know what to do. He has friends in high places. Raj doesn't know *anyone* important.'

Joyappa had heard enough. He was greatly relieved that Deepa and Raj had not identified him as the perpetrator of the hostile actions against them. However, he was a little nervous because Susheela always seemed to have a sixth sense when it came to his wrongdoings. He feared she would soon be 'on to him'. He was also slightly perplexed by Deepa's remark about the damaged Mercedes but brushed the thought aside as soon as he saw dessert being served.

Joyappa felt refreshed after lunch. Susheela, on the other hand, bore a striking resemblance to a wilted plant. The effect of the illicit pills had worn off and listening to Deepa's problems and whining had further exhausted her. She decided to spend the remainder of the day resting in the bungalow.

While driving back, Susheela told Joyappa, 'I feel so bad for that nice young couple, Deepa and Raj. I saw the poor girl sobbing and tried to console her. Apparently, Deepa's father is a wealthy businessman, and she is worried that his enemies are trying to harm them. I really don't know what the world is coming to, Joy.'

'Yes, Susheela, there are some bad people in the world,' said Joyappa, before starting to whistle loudly and tunelessly in an effort to terminate the conversation.

Susheela felt slightly better, but not well enough to attend the social. She was reading an English murder mystery while sitting up in bed and nursing a cup of hot cocoa. Joyappa was reluctant to attend the 'social' that evening, especially as Venky and Sameer weren't sure if they would be able to participate. He had no great desire to spend an evening mingling with uninteresting parents or academics. Yet, the thought of Susheela's promise to let him spend a few days 'overseas' with his friends, motivated him to gird his loins and change into formal clothes.

'Be sure to socialize, Joy,' Susheela said as she took a sip of her cocoa. 'Don't be a wallflower. You must interact with the faculty. You never know when it might be useful for Timmy's career,' she instructed.

Joyappa grunted in a non-committal manner. *What does the woman want from me?* he thought. He had agreed to attend the function with some misgivings. Now, Susheela expected him to *actually* converse with some very boring people.

'Have fun, dear,' Susheela said as she buried her nose in her book.

Joyappa pretended not to have heard as he brushed his shoes. He was preoccupied with the thought that any sort of interaction with Deepa or Raj just might prompt them to recognize him and cause a big scene.

'And, Joy, don't dance too vigorously,' Susheela cautioned. 'I don't want that old knee injury from your hockey-playing days to flare up again. I would then have to drive us to Coorg and I'm not feeling too well myself. Maybe you can do the waltz or foxtrot with someone nice. That way, the faculty and other parents will know you have participated, and you won't hurt yourself.'

'I suppose I could do that,' Joyappa replied.

'You know, Joy,' continued Susheela, 'you could ask that nice young lady, Deepa, to dance with you. Her husband seems to have hurt himself while playing cricket and probably shouldn't exert himself. What a shame! He dresses so well and is so suave. I am sure they would have enjoyed dancing together. The poor things have had a difficult time in the Nilgiris. If you pay them some attention, I am sure it would help them lift their spirits.'

Joyappa made a hurried exit. He had turned pale and emitted an odd, croaking sound that might have elicited an immediate response from a bullfrog, if it had been in the vicinity. Fortunately, Susheela didn't notice as she had turned back to her book to determine whether it was the gardener, the butler or the new scullery maid who had stabbed Lady Gwyneth.

The formal dinner and dance were to be held at the headmaster's residence—a stately, sprawling colonial-era building surrounded by a superb English garden. The headmaster and his wife, a timid-looking woman with her hair tied in a bun, stood near the entrance to welcome their guests.

Joyappa felt a twinge of embarrassment that he had crushed the poor man's hand at their first meeting. He resolved to shake his hand very gently this time. While Joyappa slowly made his way up the driveway with other parents, the headmaster inexplicably took his wife by the arm and disappeared, leaving his housekeeper to show the guests into the house. Joyappa saw the hosts vanish and shrugged. He thought there would be other opportunities in the course of the evening to be friendly with them.

When Joyappa entered the house, several parents who had participated in the cricket match or witnessed his heroics, greeted him warmly. On its own volition, Joyappa's chest swelled with pride, and his prominent rear end jutted out. *Perhaps the evening wouldn't be too bad after all*, he thought.

As he strutted about sporting a smile loaded with false modesty, Joyappa spotted Deepa and Raj. The couple were standing in a corner deep in conversation with a man wearing a bow tie and thick glasses, who had 'faculty' written all over him. Joyappa quickly slipped into another room that was also filled with people. He heard a group discussing mutual funds and tax-free bonds, and wondered if he could escape through the back door before he was bored to death.

Joyappa then heard someone in another group mention something about 'blue chips', and his curiosity was piqued. He was on the verge of butting in to ask if the chips were made of a special variety of potato or were merely infused with food colouring. He remembered seeing young plants turn purple when they didn't get enough water, but he had never seen a blue potato. However, before he could pose this profound question, he spotted Venky and Sameer conversing in a corner.

Joyappa was overjoyed to see his friends. They greeted him warmly and explained that they too had been forced by their wives to attend the function. While Venky's wife had a severe migraine, Sameer's better half had to leave for home, as her mother had suddenly taken ill. They spent a few minutes reliving their memorable victory over the school cricket team and feeling proud about the achievement. Joyappa complimented Sameer on being a superb twelfth man, and meant every word, as he had found the drinks most agreeable. Deep into the conversation, Venky said, 'Can you believe, guys, that our host, that cheapskate, couldn't spring for some booze despite the enormous fees we are paying?'

'Are you *serious*?' asked Joyappa, looking crestfallen.

'Not to worry, fellows,' Sameer said with a wink. 'I've got this superb French brandy in a few hip flasks stowed away in my pockets. All we have to do is slink into the garden when no one is looking and chug it down. There's no other way to survive a whole evening with these bores.'

The three friends soon slipped into the garden, and, in a dark area away from prying eyes, savoured the contents of Sameer's flasks. Venky and Joyappa decided that Sameer had indeed not exaggerated about the quality of the liquor.

They returned when the dinner gong sounded. Guests were ushered into a large, low-ceilinged hall. Several dining tables covered with spotless white tablecloths had been placed in the room. Colourful cut flowers in polished brass vases, placed at the centre of the tables, provided a pleasing contrast and added to the ambience.

Joyappa watched Deepa and Raj seat themselves at a table with some parents. He then led his friends to a table situated at a safe distance from them and chose a seat such that his back was to Deepa.

The food was excellent and the friends did justice to the meal. Other parents and faculty at the table were astounded at the quantity of food that was being consumed. Although too polite to stare, they did cast surreptitious glances at the three men. Joyappa's table also elicited curious looks from the other diners who noticed the steady stream of food being delivered there by harried waiters. Raj observed Joyappa's plate being loaded by a waiter for the third time, and shuddered as he remembered seeing his teammate's 'undergarments' and rash in the locker room before the cricket match. He thought of the consequences of all that food, and, with his appetite effectively destroyed, he pushed away the lettuce and bean sprouts he had been nibbling.

As they awaited dessert, Sameer told a risqué joke that had Joyappa and Venky burst out with loud laughter. By the time they finished wiping their tears, the pals were quite surprised to find they had the table to themselves.

The headmaster gave a short after-dinner speech, thanking everyone for attending the evening's function, and making yet another appeal for donations. Then, he led the way to the large ballroom, panelled with Burma teak and lit by antique chandeliers and invited everyone to dance to the music of the school orchestra.

'Fellows,' said Venky, 'I can't take any more of this formal stuff. Sameer, if you've got any of that splendid brandy hidden on your person, let's escape from here and finish it in the garden.'

Sameer, twelfth man extraordinaire, was more than happy to oblige. With the first notes from the orchestra, the three friends sneaked out to the garden, and made short work of the remaining liquor. To his companions' great pleasure, Sameer then produced three cigars that provided a superb finish to a magnificent meal.

As Joyappa flicked the ash from his cigar into a bed of hollyhocks, he heard a familiar tune wafting out of the ballroom and felt a tremendous urge to shake a leg. He also remembered that Susheela had asked him to be sociable and participate in the dance.

'I guessh Shusheelash wish ish my command,' he mumbled.

'What?' asked Venky, a little puzzled.

Joyappa attempted to repeat his statement but found the tongue twister too challenging. So, he restricted himself to, 'Letsh dansh, guysh' as he led his friends back to the elegant ballroom.

He surveyed the dance floor and saw several couples, including the headmaster and his wife, waltzing gracefully to the music. He suddenly felt a tap on the shoulder and turned to find an attractive young woman smiling up at him.

'Hello, there. I've been meaning to speak with you.'

Joyappa smiled. He recalled meeting the teacher who had guided Timmy on his botany project and been so pleasant to him. She appeared to be much more glamourous than he remembered; she was attired in a form-fitting dress and her glossy hair cascaded down to her shoulders.

'I watched you play cricket. I know I should have been rooting for the school team, but you were just superb. The way you finished the match was outstanding. You must be very strong.'

'Thank you very much, Ma'am,' Joyappa said as he racked his brain to remember her name. He hoped the letter 's' didn't feature in it, as it was bound to accentuate his slurred speech.

'Oh, please don't be so formal. Just call me Neena.'

'Okay, Neena,' said Joyappa, greatly relieved. 'Why don't you call me Joy?'

'What a lovely, happy name,' said Neena Berg. 'I also wanted to compliment you on your fielding. It was so clever. Your son must take after you. If Timmy needs any recommendations in the future or any assistance after he leaves school, you only have to ask. I think that young man has an aptitude for science and will go far.'

'Very kind of you,' Joyappa said as he carefully enunciated every word and assiduously avoided words featuring the dreaded letter that followed 'r' and preceded 't' in the alphabetical order. He decided that he could not relay the 'going far' bit to Timmy's mother in case it triggered another nervous breakdown (since Susheela appeared to be traumatized by the mere thought of her little boy living abroad).

When the orchestra started to play again after a brief interval, Neena said, 'I love that tune. Would you dance with me, Joy?'

Joyappa was a little nervous as his coordination after imbibing the brandy wasn't at its best and he didn't want to step on this nice woman's toes. As they danced the foxtrot, he found that Neena was light on her feet, and a very skilful dancer. He began to relax and enjoy the music. However, his knee suddenly locked up in the middle of the 'promenade' step. Struggling to maintain his balance, Joyappa inadvertently swept his partner off her feet. Neena was surprised but giggled and blushed prettily as she found herself suspended in Joyappa's arms. Fortunately, Joyappa's knee loosened up and they were able to finish the dance.

As Neena gracefully exited the dance floor, a young chemist, one among the many, smitten by her, said in a fit of jealousy, 'My gosh! I think the "Ice Berg" is melting. I don't think I've ever seen her smile at *anyone* before.'

'You know global warming can alter the way plants behave, even *Lactuca*,' responded his equally jealous, bespectacled colleague from the biology department.

Joyappa was now on a roll and enjoying himself. He waited until the orchestra played a tune suitable for his purpose. He then summoned Venky and Sameer, and said, 'Join me for the *Paamb Aatu*.'

He explained that this dance was meant to mimic the movements of a snake. He placed his hands, palms outward, on his forehead to resemble the hood of an Indian cobra and proceeded to dance. The sinuous, graceful movements of a snake were hard to approximate by the paunchy men, yet they tried gamely to follow Joyappa's lead.

Attracted by the writhing, swaying movements of the snake dance, the parents joined in one by one, followed by some of the younger faculty. Soon, almost everyone was on the dance floor; apparently having the time of their lives. Deepa, Raj and some of the senior faculty members, who believed that the ballroom should only be used for formal dancing, looked aghast.

The headmaster, who had decreed that only 'couples' should be on the dance floor, was absolutely horrified at the turn of events. He was torn between enforcing his rules and his dread of having to confront the evidently insane person who was now dancing like a sweaty, intoxicated, overweight cobra. He looked at his knuckles, still sore from shaking the madman's hand a few days earlier, and swiftly decided that it would be safer not to intervene. He prayed that the strange dance would soon be over and normalcy would return.

Unfortunately for the headmaster, before the orchestra finished playing the piece, Joyappa weaved his way up to the conductor and whispered something in his ear. The conductor, a teacher of Western classical music, nodded and smiled. In all his years of service, he had never witnessed the participants having so much fun. He decided that the evening was definitely taking an interesting turn.

As soon as the music started to play once more, Joyappa sat down on his haunches, and the other dancers followed his lead. He then proceeded to do the '*Kappe Aatu*' or the Frog Dance, during which he jumped around like an amphibian. Given his dodgy knee, Joyappa had to quit in a few minutes, but he watched proudly as his protégés hopped around on the elegant ballroom floor, while the orchestra managed to play some sort of choppy music that worked superbly for the dance.

The music teacher too was enjoying himself. He was certain that the staid ballroom had never previously been the site of such unbridled exuberance. Joyappa, lathered in sweat, was quite exhausted. So, he bade Venky and Sameer goodbye after promising to meet them next year, and quietly left the headmaster's residence. As he drove back to the bungalow, he felt quite satisfied with himself. He had attended the event. He had danced and interacted with the faculty and parents. Surely, he reasoned, Susheela *could not* find fault with his actions.

Susheela was up early the following morning. She was feeling better physically, but the thought of being apart from Timmy for several months left her feeling blue. She felt relieved that Joyappa was there to drive her back to Coorg, as she would not be able to focus on the long drive down the steep 'ghats', with numerous hairpin bends.

Joyappa was fast asleep, so she shook him awake and said, 'Get up Joy, we have a long drive ahead of us and I'd like to say bye to Timmy before we leave.'

Joyappa groaned. 'Everything hurts, Susheela. Everything,' he said with a whimper.

Susheela was concerned. 'What happened? You were quite okay last evening.'

'You asked me to dance at the social, Susheela. So, I did. Now, I am in pain. Pain in my knee, pain in my back, pain everywhere,' he croaked.

'I'm sorry, Joy,' Susheela was immediately contrite. 'I should have considered your old knee injury and shouldn't have insisted that you dance.'

'Pain in my head, pain in my thighs…' moaned Joyappa, piteously.

'Wait a minute,' Susheela interrupted him. 'You didn't have too much to drink, did you?'

Joyappa sat up and looked at her accusingly. 'Susheela, you know that alcohol is forbidden by the school. None was served. What more can I say?'

'Of course, Joy. I'm sorry. Well, I guess I'll drive down and wish Timmy goodbye. Meanwhile, please get ready, dear.'

'Okay, Susheela. Thanks, and I'm sorry I'm not feeling too well. Please wish Timmy for me.'

'Don't worry. You can rest, dear. I shall drive us back to Coorg.'

While Susheela was away at school, Joyappa quickly stuffed himself with a massive breakfast, which Abraham brought him, as soon as Susheela drove out of the gate. He crammed his belongings in a suitcase and generously tipped the staff of the bungalow as they had made his stay most comfortable. Then Joyappa waited for Susheela.

When Susheela returned, she looked sad but composed. As Joyappa walked towards the car, he exaggerated his limp and rubbed his back. He hoped these actions would elicit some sympathy and he could nap peacefully in the car. He wanted Susheela neither to talk to him about how sad she was feeling nor ask him to take the wheel on the gruelling drive back home.

Joyappa knew Susheela was a competent driver who drove much more cautiously than him. By the time they drove out of Ooty and began the steep descent to the plains, Joyappa was snoring gently, even as Susheela skilfully negotiated the treacherous hairpin bends. When they reached Masinagudi, he thought he heard a little sniffling, but deliberately kept his eyes closed fearing the start of a conversation that might trigger a cascade of tears. In fact, he tried to snore a little louder to drown out the melancholic sounds.

After passing a couple of game sanctuaries, Joyappa felt thirsty and requested Susheela to stop the car. As she felt somewhat remorseful about forcing Joyappa to dance, and thereby trigger his old knee injury, Susheela was most solicitous. She came around to the passenger's side and helped Joyappa out of the car. She seated him in the shade of a tamarind tree, bought a tender coconut from the vendor by the side of the road and carried it to him. When he was done, she had the coconut sliced open. The vendor scooped out the tender flesh and Susheela carried it to Joyappa. After the first coconut, he decided he liked the unusual attention.

So, in a weak voice, he said, 'Susheela, I hate to bother you. But, do you think I could have one more?'

'Sure, Joy. Just a second,' said Susheela, as she quickly trotted off to the vendor.

When they resumed their journey, Susheela asked Joyappa about the dinner and dance. He answered with a mixture of obfuscation, some truth and numerous lies. He told Susheela that the food was just 'okay'. He claimed to have only consumed lettuce and sprouts. He told her that he had danced with someone whose name he couldn't recall. He said she was a rather unattractive, overweight member of the faculty who sported several long hairs on her upper lip. He added that she was very clumsy and couldn't dance half as well as Susheela.

'Joy,' Susheela rebuked him sternly, 'you should not describe people as unattractive and overweight. It is very unkind.'

'Susheela, I really missed you last evening. I had to force myself to dance as you had asked me to be sociable. But it was no fun. I'm sorry if I said disrespectful things about that teacher. I know I shouldn't be comparing people, but I just blurted out what was on my mind because I was thinking about how well you dance and how pretty you are,' said Joyappa in a small voice.

'It's nice of you to say that about me, Joy. But you really should be more sensitive,' Susheela replied.

Joyappa promised to be more respectful while describing people. He also mentioned that he had spoken to several members of the faculty and they were all willing to help Timmy. He slyly added that the reason they were so helpful was because Timmy's mother was charming and a great cross-country runner. He concluded by saying that the headmaster was very cordial and asked them to visit any time they were in the Nilgiris.

Susheela listened to Joyappa, but, as her senses had been dulled by the pills and the sorrow of parting from her 'Timmykins', she couldn't quite sift through the information and identify the untruths and half-truths in Joyappa's story with her customary efficiency.

On the outskirts of Mysore, where the 'mobile' signal was strong, Susheela's phone pinged many times. She pulled over and took a few minutes to read the text and download the images as Joyappa daydreamed about the grand vacation he was going to have with his friends 'overseas' in Goa.

There seemed to be something different about Susheela when she restarted the car. There was a tightness around her mouth as she floored the accelerator and drove with hitherto unseen aggression. She hit the brakes hard and often, and each time, Joyappa's injured knee banged violently against the dashboard, causing him to squeal.

At lunch time, much to Joyappa's disappointment, she stopped at a 'Pure Vegetarian' restaurant. She didn't help him out of the car and much to his dismay, ordered him a small bowl of curds. After the sparse meal, Susheela asked Joyappa for his wallet saying she needed some money to settle the bill. She extracted most of the currency leaving him with less than one hundred rupees in smaller denomination notes before returning the wallet.

Joyappa was perplexed at the sudden change in Susheela's mood, but he chose to keep silent, as he knew an explanation would soon be forthcoming. Sure enough, a few minutes later, Susheela said, 'Joy, I need to show you something. Deepa and I exchanged phone numbers and she just sent me some images from the headmaster's house.'

Joyappa gulped. He knew he was in for it. The first image on the screen showed Joyappa and several others on their haunches performing the *Kappe Aatu* or Frog Dance, while the headmaster and a couple of older faculty members looked on in horror. The second image showed the lovely Ms Neena Berg, with an adoring expression on her face (that clearly lacked excess facial hair), suspended in Joyappa's arms. The third image showed a perspiring Joyappa leading a group of dancers doing the *Paamb Aatu* or snake dance.

'Joy, is that woman in your arms the unattractive moustached woman you described?'

'Umm, yes,' Joyappa said, tentatively. 'She's terribly, terribly unattractive. Well, I meant compared to you, honeybunny,' he added.

Susheela didn't dignify his answer with a reply. Instead, she said, 'I can understand now why your knee and the rest of your body are feeling sore. You went and performed those odd manoeuvres rather than sticking to ballroom dancing. I have *no* sympathy for you, Joy. Absolutely none whatsoever!'

'But, Susheela,' whined Joyappa, who was still hung over and experiencing aches in different parts of his head from Susheela's verbal assault. 'You asked me to go to the dance,' he blurted out in a vain bid to apportion blame.

Susheela looked at him coldly and said, 'I am driving home, Joy. I have left you just enough money to take a bus. So, don't go and squander it or you will have to walk back. I hope this will serve as a lesson that you must never, ever lie to me.'

Susheela marched off towards the parking lot in a huff. The young couple at the next table pretended not to stare as they stopped eating their large, wafer thin dosas.

'I suppose she's in Angri-La,' muttered Joyappa to himself.

Joyappa looked at the meagre amount left in his wallet and wondered if he had enough money to get a nice, crisp masala dosa before enquiring about the next bus home. When he realized that Susheela had left him just enough cash for buying a ticket on the slow, uncomfortable 'shuttle' bus, he decided that he could still outsmart her by calling his friend Chomu, who would certainly come to his rescue. Maybe they could hit one of their favourite bars before loading up on a variety of barbecued meats at 'Grills without Frills'.

Unfortunately, for Joyappa, in the nanosecond before he could speed dial Chomu, Susheela came storming back, snatched his phone and said through clenched teeth, 'Not so fast, Joy. I'm taking that with me, you big, fat liar!'

'But, but, Susheela,' Joyappa could only splutter, shell-shocked at her reappearance and his ruined plans.

'When you are on that bus, think about mending your ways, Joy. I can't believe you told me that you danced with an unattractive woman, when she could easily pass for a movie star or a model. Everything you said was a lie. You are such a snake!'

After Susheela left, Joyappa figured he must have done something right on the dance floor if Susheela actually thought he *was* a snake.

'I hope she meant a majestic cobra, though, not some shy rat snake or wolf snake,' he muttered.

3

The Killjoys

Joyappa was not happy. Susheela's Aunt Poovie and Uncle Jappoo were visiting from somewhere in the northern part of the country, where they had settled after Jappoo sold his successful garment business.

Joyappa's discontent was not merely the outcome of his routine being disrupted. The visitors had no children of their own and doted upon Susheela. Conversely, Joyappa got the distinct impression that the couple viewed him with the same affection they might bestow on pond scum. Upon arrival, they showered Susheela with expensive gifts, whereas all Joyappa received was a second hand, curry-stained book titled, *How to Lose Weight and Gain Friends*. Both Poovie and Jappoo were somewhat plump, and, in his opinion, not 'friend-magnets'. So, Joyappa was certain they had not read it themselves.

Joyappa was not particularly offended by the book, which he was never going to read anyway. He even tolerated not being able to watch his favourite television shows from his comfortable couch, which now seemed to be perpetually occupied by the guests. What really got Joyappa's goat were the lectures. Poovie and Jappoo had found religion late in life and they had turned to it in a big way. Consequently, they were constantly 'preaching'.

One evening, after a long day on the coffee estate, Joyappa sprawled out on his couch, eager to watch an international hockey match on television. He was happy to find himself alone in the room. His cats, Tiny and Bug, sneaked into the room, hopped onto his lap and began to purr as he stroked them. The match was exciting, and the teams were evenly matched. The Indian team was performing well and had just taken the lead. Engrossed in the game, Joyappa wasn't aware that anyone had entered the room until he felt a tap on his shoulder. He looked up to find Susheela and the guests standing by the couch.

'Oh, Joy,' said Susheela, 'would you be a dear and watch your show some other time. Uncle and Aunty are keen to watch that American preacher they were telling me about. I guess he's on right now. I'm going to be busy in the kitchen, so you need to keep them company for a while.'

Joyappa grunted unhappily but didn't bother to explain that his 'show', poised at an exciting stage, would not be on 'some other time'. Jappoo instructed him to flip to a channel that ostensibly focussed on matters spiritual. Joyappa, unaware that such a channel even existed on television, obliged. A large, silver-haired man with a booming voice appeared on the screen; he was telling the somewhat scared-looking congregation about the unspeakable things that were bound to happen to them in the afterlife if they sinned.

Poovie's face was imbued with divine fervour as she watched the preacher raise both his arms dramatically and look skywards. Jappoo kept looking at Joyappa with a weird, expectant look on his face. Joyappa knew *exactly* what Jappoo wanted—which was to displace Joyappa and occupy the comfortable couch—but pretended not to notice as he continued to scratch Tiny under her chin.

When Susheela entered the room, she was surprised to see the guests still standing. Jappoo, pleased to see her pull up a tiny stool, rudely motioned Joyappa to get off the couch. Joyappa was annoyed but decided to tolerate the discomfort as the guests were due to leave the following day. However, the seat of the stool was considerably narrower than Joyappa's substantial posterior; consequently, a large portion of his rear remained unsupported and hung over the edges. Even the cats were restless as they could not curl up comfortably on Joyappa, who was continually shifting his position on the tiny seat to maintain his perch. They glared at him and eventually leapt off to exact their revenge by sneaking into his bedroom and shredding the latest edition of his favourite sports magazine.

For a quarter of an hour, Joyappa marvelled at the behaviour of his guests, as they occupied his favourite couch and stared at the screen. He noticed that they often exchanged glances and beatific smiles with each other. They even clapped noisily, while they observed the large man flapping his arms and promising eternal happiness to his followers if they would accept his direction.

Finally, the show was over. As the closing credits filled the screen, a relieved Joyappa reached out to retrieve the television remote and return to the match. Poovie, however, had other ideas. Just as Joyappa's fingers closed over the device, she grabbed it and quickly pressed the numbers of the channel *she* wanted. A smug-looking bearded man clad in flowing robes appeared on the screen, chanting in a language that Joyappa could not understand.

'Excellent,' Jappoo said, giving a pleased look to Poovie.

Joyappa was terribly upset to miss the concluding part of the hockey match. He had to exercise all his self-control to keep from immobilizing Jappoo in a headlock and smothering Poovie with a pillow.

To sublimate these unkind thoughts, and given Poovie and Jappoo's religious inclinations, Joyappa decided to secretly refer to them as 'Poo-Ja'. He was quite pleased with the moniker. He felt he was just as creative as the members of the paparazzi who renamed celebrity couples by amalgamating their names and treating them as a single entity. He chuckled at his own wit but knew that he dare not share the joke with Susheela.

Just when Joyappa thought he could neither endure the religious shows nor tolerate his guests any longer, a delicious fragrance wafted into the room. He sniffed the air like a hunting dog and immediately felt uplifted as he rightly concluded that Susheela had cooked a mutton pot roast for dinner. He loved the way Susheela prepared the dish—delicately flavoured, with the tender meat falling off the bone.

'Yum, yum, yum,' muttered Joyappa, with heartfelt delight.

'Om, om, om,' chanted 'Poo-Ja', even more joyfully.

When Susheela rang the dinner gong, which Joyappa thought to be rather pretentious— she only did this when they had company—they all trooped into the dining room. Joyappa eyed the pot roast and rubbed his hands in anticipation.

'Looks delicious, Sushie,' said Poovie.

'I know,' Jappoo said, smiling at Susheela. 'You are so talented, sweetie.'

'Thank you,' Susheela said, blushing. 'I just hope you like it.'

As Susheela moved to serve Poovie, Jappoo raised his hand and said, 'Hold on, would you Sushie? I think we should say a little prayer.'

The next five minutes were pure agony for Joyappa, as he stared at the pot roast while 'Poo-Ja' chanted something in what was possibly Sanskrit, or perhaps Latin, he could not quite tell. When it was finally over, Susheela served the guests generous helpings of the pot roast, with mashed potatoes on the side.

Joyappa eagerly reached for the pot to serve himself but was devastated when Susheela said, 'Oh, Joy, that's not for you. You may have some mashed potatoes, but I don't think the roast is good for you, especially as you need to go to Mysore for your medical tests. Instead, I've baked some nice soy cubes for you, dear.'

Joyappa was crushed. His bad mood worsened as he tried to chew the bland, rubbery soy cubes while watching the guests relish every morsel.

'Oh, this is absolutely delicious, Sushie. You must give me your recipe. I just love the way the meat falls off the bone,' said Poovie.

'I agree,' Jappoo said. 'This is superb, Sushie. Mmmm, just perfect flavour, and the meat is incredibly tender. I love it,' he added.

'I am so glad you like the pot roast. Please help yourself to more and finish it. Joy shouldn't be eating anything rich, and if there are any leftovers, you can rest assured he will gobble them up when no one is watching,' Susheela said with a laugh.

The guests' incessant chatter made the meal even more intolerable for Joyappa. After they had praised the food for the umpteenth time, they proceeded to say the most boring things imaginable (in Joyappa's opinion).

'You know, Sushie. I've been reading this great book titled, *Harmony and Peace in the Universe*,' said Poovie.

'Hmmm, excellent book,' Jappoo agreed, before pausing to detach a succulent piece of flesh from a marrow bone. He loaded his fork with the meat, smeared on some mashed potatoes and closed his eyes as he chewed and swallowed with a look of sheer rapture plastered on his face.

Poovie continued, 'The author says that every atom, every molecule and every living being is connected by a divine thread. If only everyone realized this, there would be no aggression, disagreements, fights or wars. Love, pure unadulterated love, for our fellow beings is the answer. Particularly those of us who have the means and the required higher consciousness *must* care for the animals, the poor and the downtrodden as if they are a part of our own being.

Jappoo picked up a marrow spoon and scooped out the contents of the bone onto his plate, 'Mmmm. Aaaah,' he exclaimed as he gulped down the marrow with a look of bliss. He carefully fished out the last two pieces of meat from the pot and placed one on Poovie's plate before serving himself. Susheela excused herself and headed to the kitchen to put the finishing touches on the dessert she had prepared.

Joyappa picked at the insipid soy cubes on his plate and sadly listened to the varied sounds of enjoyment emanating from the couple. Finally, they were done. Several gleaming bones, picked absolutely clean, served as the only evidence of the meal. Poovie and Jappoo then pushed back their chairs and dabbed at their mouths simultaneously, reminding Joyappa of the coordination displayed by the gold-medal winning synchronized swimmers during the last Olympics.

'That was magnificent. I haven't had a better meal since we had lobster in Maine a couple of years ago,' Jappoo reminisced.

'Nothing like boiling something alive to show your love,' muttered Joyappa under his breath.

'As I was saying,' Jappoo continued, 'respecting and loving each other is the only way forward.'

'You are right, dear. We must love and respect everyone and everything in the universe', Poovie said. Then she gave Joyappa a stern look and said, 'Jay, why don't you help Sushie? That poor thing has been slaving for hours to feed us. I think it would behove you to clear the table and make it easier for her. She is such a treasure.'

Joyappa fought the urge to stuff the soy cubes into every visible orifice of 'Poo-Ja' to silence this awful, two-headed entity. However, better sense prevailed and he grudgingly complied with the request. With all that talk of love and respect, he wondered why they did not show him enough respect to at least get his name right. *And what normal person uses words like 'behove'? What the heck did it mean, anyway?* he thought.

'Oh, Jay,' said Jappoo, 'We would like some warm water on your way back from the kitchen. But make sure it isn't *too* hot, mind you. Oh, and a couple of toothpicks would be nice, boy.'

Joyappa quietly went into the kitchen, where he saw that Susheela had put together a hot-fudge sundae with home-made ice cream. It looked wonderful, but he knew that he would have to be content with a banana or an apple for dessert. He decided not to prolong his agony. He informed Susheela that he had to make an urgent phone call with regard to some irrigation requirements and escaped to the garage.

Joyappa had stashed a quarter bottle of rum under a particularly dirty and greasy tarpaulin that he was sure Susheela would not touch. As he reflected upon the evening, he bravely attempted to erase the memories of the more traumatic parts by indulging in a bit of 'irrigation'.

Susheela had instructed Joyappa to drop Poovie and Jappoo at the railway station in Mysore early the following morning before going for his medical tests. Joyappa did not look forward to the conversation he would have to endure during the journey but was relieved that he would be rid of the couple after this final wretched session with them.

The next day, Joyappa woke up early. He entered the dining room to find Poovie and Jappoo eating a breakfast of omelettes stuffed with wild mushrooms and cherry tomatoes. Susheela had supplemented the main dish with bagels and cream cheese.

The food looked and smelled so delicious that Joyappa didn't feel even a tinge of annoyance when the guests said, 'Good morning, Jay,' in unison without even glancing at him. Joyappa observed that there was no boring porridge at his place on the table. He rubbed his hands together in anticipation as he waited for Susheela to bring out one of her special omelettes for him. But when Susheela breezed into the dining room, all she brought was a steaming pot of coffee.

'What a great way to start the day, Sushie,' Poovie said. 'Those wild mushrooms really add flavour to the omelette. It was so clever of you to use cherry tomatoes, dear. I just love that nutty flavour.'

'Everything is perfect, dear,' Jappoo agreed as he spread a generous amount of cream cheese on an onion bagel. 'Poovie, we should take Sushie with us. She is such a treasure. I have to say Jay is one lucky, lucky chap.'

'Thanks, Uncle. That is so sweet of you,' Susheela said with a smile. Then she turned to Joyappa and remarked sternly, 'Joy, what exactly are you doing at the table? Please remember, your lab tests are long overdue. You are not to eat anything until after the technician has drawn your blood for analysis.'

'Aarggh,' Joyappa growled, unhappily.

'Ha ha,' Jappoo said, as he buttered another bagel, 'I guess he forgot, Sushie. He doesn't know what he's missing. What a superb breakfast!'

'Sushie,' Poovie said, pausing to take a sip of freshly brewed coffee. 'Have you considered entering one of those reality shows for cooks? Oh my gosh, this is heavenly, sweetie.'

'Jay,' said Jappoo. 'As you aren't eating, be a good chap and bring the bags down from our room. That ought to save us a lot of time. While you are at it, please look around and make sure I haven't left anything important, like my pants or underwear in the bathroom. If you find anything, just place it in my suitcase before you load up the car,' Jappoo instructed.

'Great idea,' said Poovie. 'Jay, if my spare dentures are in the bathroom, rinse them out carefully and pack them in the blue suitcase.'

Joyappa gritted his teeth as thoughts of extreme violence filled his mind. He had to exercise tremendous self-control to resist the urge to slam their heads together.

Mercifully, Poovie's spare dentures were not in the bathroom. Joyappa gingerly picked up a pair of orange men's briefs that were surprisingly skimpy and dazzlingly bright. He shoved them into one of the suitcases and washed his hands thoroughly. After single-handedly hauling down every piece of luggage and loading up the car, he sourly observed Jappoo and Poovie hug and kiss Susheela before inviting *her* to their place.

Following the tearful farewell, Susheela turned to Joyappa and said, 'Joy, make sure Uncle and Aunty are seated in the right compartment on the train. Don't be late.'

'Sure, Susheela,' Joyappa said with a smile, his mood much buoyed as he visualized 'Poo-Ja' being ferried to the distant northern part of the country in a superfast train.

'Oh, I forgot to mention. By the time you return, Asha will be here. I'm so glad she's visiting; it will help me cope as the house will feel so empty without Uncle and Aunty,' Susheela said, as she dabbed at her eyes.

Joyappa was devastated. *Asha! My God, Count Dracula or Cruella de Vil would be preferable!* he thought. Asha was Susheela's very snooty bosom buddy, who clearly disapproved of Joyappa and did not think he was worthy of Susheela. Joyappa guessed—his surmise was actually quite accurate—that Asha criticized him and laughed at him behind his back.

Joyappa came from hardy, warrior stock. Other than turning pale, and having his smile freeze into an awful rictus, which Susheela conveniently appeared not to notice, there was little evidence of the internal turmoil he was experiencing. He clutched at a nearby bougainvillea shrub in an effort to stay upright and didn't even feel the thorns pierce his skin. Somehow, he managed to get into the car and slowly drive away as Susheela waved and blew kisses at Poovie and Jappoo.

Mercifully, both his passengers, with their bellies full, dozed off in the back seat. Other than the sound of their gentle snoring, Joyappa was left alone with his thoughts for about half an hour. Initially, he was overcome with feelings of self-pity as he considered having to contend with Asha before he could fully recover from Poovie and Jappoo's visit. However, after the recent rains, the countryside was green and easy on the eye, and Joyappa's disposition soon improved. He began to think about what he would eat after his lab visit and started to whistle softly as he imagined gorging on gulab jamuns, dosas, wadas and many other fried delicacies that Susheela had banned from his diet.

'Hey, Jay,' Jappoo said on waking up, as Joyappa was negotiating the relatively heavy traffic in Hunsur, the rapidly expanding town located about an hour away from Mysore.

'Yes?' Joyappa queried grumpily, as his pleasant thoughts were rudely interrupted.

'Stop at that new restaurant, boy,' ordered Jappoo. 'I could do with some good, spicy southern food before we board the train. How about you, Poovie?'

'Excellent idea, dear,' said Poovie, as she rubbed her hands together in anticipation. 'Look! It's a drive-in. They provide service right up to the vehicle, so we don't even have to get out of the car.'

Almost as soon as Joyappa pulled into an empty space in the parking lot, a waiter, smartly attired in a spotless white tunic and a rather grand maroon turban, appeared before them. Poovie and Jappoo ordered exactly what Joyappa had been daydreaming about a few minutes before. The service was quick and efficient, and Joyappa began to salivate as the delicious aroma of fried food filled the car.

The sounds of Joyappa's passengers devouring their 'second breakfast', punctuated by numerous comments, including 'Oooh, that chutney is delicious, dear' and 'Mmmm, I love the crispness of that dosa, Jappsie', added to his chagrin. He concluded that this sort of torture could well induce the most resolute of spies to divulge every secret they had been trained to guard with their lives.

Joyappa was beginning to feel somewhat worried that the impromptu stop might cause his passengers to miss their train from Mysore, thereby forcing him to endure even more of their company. Luckily, the waiter was efficient and as soon as the last drop of coffee had been slurped up, he removed the dishes and presented Jappoo with the bill.

Jappoo cleared his throat meaningfully and said, 'Jay, would you be a good chap and pay the fellow? I'm going to need some cash for the journey, so I would rather not spend it here. Oh, and be sure to add a generous tip. The service was excellent, and I am a firm believer that good service must be rewarded. I just cannot stand skinflints.'

Joyappa was furious but quietly complied with the request. As they resumed their journey, all sorts of violent ideas crossed his mind. He was not well-versed with the law of the land, but he had a sneaking suspicion that flinging senior citizens out of a moving car would be a punishable offence. He resorted to gritting his teeth and gripping the steering wheel so firmly that it was in danger of breaking.

To make matters worse, Poovie and Jappoo seemed to have perked up after their nap and second breakfast; they actually started talking to Joyappa. As Joyappa did not have earplugs for himself, or socks to stuff into his passengers' mouths, he was forced to listen.

Poovie said, 'Jay, we are really going to miss Sushie. She is such a darling. We had once hoped she would marry a doctor or a business tycoon.'

'Hmm,' Joyappa growled.

'But unfortunately…' Poovie added, with a shrug. She looked at Joyappa meaningfully as she cleared her throat but did not complete the thought.

'You are one lucky fellow, Jay. I hope you are taking care of that girl. Say, are you still drinking like a fish?' Jappoo asked.

Joyappa hadn't actually observed a fish drinking, so he was slightly tentative when he said, 'Nope, I'm not.'

'Good. We were very disappointed to hear that you were a

drunkard, or alcoholic, or whatever the modern term is these days,' Jappoo said.

'Remember your body is like a temple. You must look after it well,' Poovie added.

'If you are healthy, you will be happy. When you are happy, your whole being will be suffused with love. Love is what will save this universe, Jay. You must be a loving husband to our Sushie. Only love will make you a better husband and father. Believe me, if you treat everyone and every living being with love and respect, you will feel a divine connection with the entire universe,' Jappoo preached.

Just then a scrawny looking stray dog bolted across the road, and Joyappa swerved sharply to avoid it. The tyres squealed, leaving a trail of burnt rubber on the tar road. Fortunately, there was no harm done. Joyappa wiped his brow in relief as the dog scampered to safety and they continued on their journey.

'Whoa, that was close!' Jappoo remarked. 'All these damn stray dogs are a public health hazard. I believe running over a few of them and euthanizing the rest would make life a lot easier for us.'

Joyappa was very fond of dogs, and he was pleased that the mongrel had escaped unscathed. He was, however, horrified at Jappoo's response, especially after being lectured not a moment ago, about treating 'every living being with love and respect'. He accelerated, knowing that missing the train would mean more of the same, and an earful from Susheela. Fortunately, traffic wasn't heavy and he was able to reach the railway station on time.

Jappoo refused to engage a porter to haul their luggage, stating that he didn't want to be exploited by 'those crooks'. So, Joyappa was compelled to carry their heavy bags to the train, find the appropriate compartment and stow it in the overhead racks.

'Now, before you leave Jay, get me a newspaper and a couple of religious books for the journey,' Jappoo directed.

When Joyappa returned to the compartment with the reading material, Jappoo grabbed the paper and immediately began to read it without any word of thanks.

'Remember, Jay,' Poovie remarked as they parted, 'you must look after Sushie well.'

'Yes, love her and cherish her,' Jappoo added without looking up from the daily horoscope listed in the paper.

Joyappa was exhausted from the lack of food, the stressful drive, unsolicited lectures and having to haul the guests' luggage. Susheela had insisted that he go to a specific, reputed laboratory in the heart of Mysore city. After negotiating the crowded, narrow roads, he was understandably irritable by the time he reached his destination. The unplanned stop in Hunsur had caused him to arrive later than he had expected. Consequently, there was a long queue snaking out of the building.

Joyappa joined the queue behind a thin man wearing a white polyester shirt and a multi-coloured lungi. Shortly, a pregnant woman with a little boy clinging to her sari came and stood behind Joyappa. The queue kept getting longer as even more people arrived. Progress was slow, and as the day became warmer, Joyappa became more anxious to be done with his tests.

As they shuffled forward, the woman behind Joyappa bumped into him with her stomach, thus causing his own large belly to brush against the man standing in front of him. Joyappa apologized, and the man turned around and smiled pleasantly, revealing nicotine-stained teeth.

'So, what are you here for?' the thin man asked.

'Oh, just some routine tests,' Joyappa replied non-committally.

The man coughed violently, hawked and expectorated into the street. 'I'm here for a tuberculosis check-up. I've been taking a course of medicines for several months and it's time for a test.'

When the man coughed again, Joyappa inadvertently took a step back and bumped into the expectant mother. He raised his hand in apology, but the woman seemed unperturbed and smiled in a friendly manner. Joyappa hated to be bumped or jostled, but clearly it wasn't an issue with those standing in the queue with him.

The pregnant woman tapped the man in front of Joyappa on his shoulder and spoke reassuringly, 'Sir, don't worry, I am sure you will be fine. My husband had TB as well, as did my in-laws, but they are all well now.'

As his neighbours in the queue exchanged notes about their ailments, Joyappa tried to make himself smaller by contorting his body to avoid any physical contact with them. He wasn't sure how tuberculosis affected the human body, or if the woman could be a carrier. However, he *was* sure that the disease was infectious and he didn't want to fall ill by inhaling dangerous germs. In an effort to breathe the cleanest air available, he stood on his toes and raised his head upwards every time he filled his lungs.

Joyappa's movements were peculiar to say the least. The people in the queue observing him became concerned, and his new acquaintances decided to act. While the pregnant woman took him by one arm, the habitually spitting TB patient held the other. Both of these kind-hearted people briskly marched Joyappa to the front of the line. They insisted to the overworked receptionist that Joyappa would need to undergo testing before anyone else, on account of his undiagnosed ailment.

Joyappa was touched by the kindness of the strangers (although he could have done without *literally* being touched). He thanked them but was not very amused when the pregnant woman's son pointed at his paunch and asked, 'Ma, is that man also going to have a baby?'

Susheela had given him a long list of tests to go through. Joyappa provided samples of whatever was required by the lab technicians. Despite the large number of people milling around, there was a system in place and everything worked efficiently. The only hiccup Joyappa faced was when a new technician misplaced his urine sample. However, she was very apologetic when she asked him to provide another one.

Joyappa was extremely hungry and quite annoyed by then. He handed the sample to the same technician, but fixed her with a fierce look and growled, 'You better not lose this one.'

'Yes Sir, I mean no Sir,' she squeaked as she placed the sample in a tray with trembling hands.

'Tell me your name,' Joyappa demanded.

'It, it is Ve…Vee…Veena, Sir,' stuttered the terrified young woman, whose first day of work was turning out to be a nightmare. College hadn't prepared her to deal with large, irate men.

'Don't botch this, Ve Vee Veena,' Joyappa said to the rattled technician, before adding, 'Strange name, indeed. Did your parents actually name you that?'

Joyappa was ravenous and left before Veena could answer. Following a hearty breakfast, he returned to the laboratory at the assigned time to provide more bodily fluids for analysis. As Susheela had insisted on various other scans and tests, Joyappa dutifully jumped through the hoops. When he was finally done, he informed the receptionist that he would not be able to pick up the results in person and requested her to send them to Susheela's e-mail address instead.

It had been a stressful day. Just as Joyappa was getting ready to drive to his favourite watering hole in the city to relax and ease his tensions, his phone rang. When he saw it was Susheela, his first thought was of ignoring the call—at least until after he had hit the bar. But within the first couple of rings, he relented and decided to answer in case it was an emergency.

'Joy,' Susheela said, 'if you are done with the tests, would you please go to a supermarket and pick up some essentials. It is urgent. I'm going to send you a message with a list of what I need. Pick up everything and head back right away. Asha is due any time now and there's hardly anything at home.'

'Hmm,' Joyappa replied, struggling to come up with a plausible lie that would first let him enjoy a drink before doing the shopping.

'Oh, pleeaase Joy,' Susheela pleaded. 'I will cook you some extra spicy pandi curry and crisp *akki otti*, just the way you like, if you arrive soon.'

The offer was tempting, but so was a nice cold beer. Joyappa didn't answer right away, as he was still thinking of ways to satisfy his craving without getting into trouble.

Susheela, who possessed an uncanny ability to read his mind, said, 'I picked up some of that excellent Mountain Spring beer from a microbrewery in Ooty, Joy. I was saving it for a special occasion. If you get here soon, I'm certain you will enjoy it with your meal.'

'Okay, Susheela, I guess I'll be there shortly,' Joyappa replied. He did, indeed, rate Mountain Spring beer highly and decided to accept Susheela's offer.

4

Good News!

Joyappa picked up the groceries on his list and swiftly drove back home from Mysore. He anticipated a delicious, home-cooked meal after the sparse fare Susheela had been serving him lately.

Joyappa entered the house through the back door and stepped into the kitchen. He was disappointed not to find Susheela cooking the meal she had promised him. The grocery list had unusual ingredients and products that he knew nothing about, so rather than putting them away in the wrong place, he unloaded the car and left them in the pantry for Susheela.

When Joyappa stepped into the sitting room, hoping to find Susheela, he turned pale. She was not there either. Instead, there was someone else reading a fashion magazine in the corner. He had completely forgotten about Asha's arrival in his excitement to get to the meal and special beer Susheela had promised him.

'Oh, hello, Joy,' Asha said, lowering the glossy magazine.

'Hello, hello, hello, 'Joyappa responded nervously.

Asha looked a little different to him since he had last seen her. Her makeup was perfect and she was fashionably attired, as always. But her hair had been styled and coloured differently, and she appeared to have lost a lot of weight.

'You look well,' he added, not really meaning it. Joyappa thought the skeleton he had seen in his son's biology laboratory looked plump in comparison.

'As do you,' said Asha as she looked him up and down, taking in the five o'clock shadow, the rumpled, sweat-stained clothes and his paunch. She raised an eyebrow and he sensed that she was mocking him.

Joyappa became nervous under the scrutiny. 'Siddown, siddown, Asha,' he urged the already seated woman.

Asha smiled revealing white, perfect teeth as she raised both eyebrows. The smile didn't reach her eyes, and Joyappa knew she was enjoying his discomfiture.

Joyappa backed out of the room to look for Susheela, who he found in the vegetable garden harvesting some exotic herbs. 'Hey, I didn't find you in the kitchen. I'm starving. How's that curry coming along?' he asked expectantly.

'Hi, Joy, I didn't hear you come home. Ash is on a special diet, so I decided we would just have a salad today, dear,' Susheela said. 'Besides, we ought to wait until the results of your tests come in before you can have pork. You know how much fat that meat has, and we wouldn't want your cholesterol and other parameters to spike, would we?'

'But, you promised,' whined Joyappa.

'There, there, Joy,' Susheela said soothingly. 'I didn't say I'd cook you *pandi* curry *today,* dear. Let's wait until Asha leaves. We can't very well serve a rich, fatty dish when she's on such a strict diet. By the way, doesn't she look lovely?'

'No fair,' Joyappa said, as he pouted and stamped his foot on the ground like a little boy, 'What about the beer you promised?'

'I assumed we'd wait for your test results for that, too. I promise you can have your beer with your special meal, Joy,'

Susheela placated him, as she carried an armful of some green leafy stuff indoors, leaving Joyappa pouting and fuming outside.

Joyappa had a sneaking suspicion—certainly well-founded—that Susheela had cunningly engineered the whole grocery shopping incident to prevent him from indulging in rich food and liquor while he was 'unsupervised' in Mysore. He fervently hoped his test results would not cause any further dietary restrictions.

Dinner was eminently unsatisfying to Joyappa. Asha and Susheela chattered on about diets, carbohydrates, proteins, fats (both saturated and unsaturated) vitamins and minerals as they picked at their salads. Joyappa nibbled at the bland, green stuff in front of him and hoped dessert would be palatable. Sadly, a single pink guava was all that he got, while the women ate fat-free frozen yoghurt while discussing shoes and handbags.

Joyappa thought back about the awful journey with 'Poo-Ja', the stressful lab tests, the arrival of Asha 'de Vil' and Susheela's devious manipulations. Memories of the day's humiliating transrectal ultrasound, which he had managed to suppress, also came flooding back with a vengeance. He concluded that it had been an awful day with a few redeeming features. He consoled himself by muttering, 'Things cannot get much worse, so tomorrow is bound to be a better day.'

The following morning, Joyappa found a note on the dining table by his porridge bowl. The first part of the note stated that Susheela and Asha had already left for an early run. Joyappa marvelled at the women's obsession with their weight. He mumbled to himself, 'If people lose weight from jogging, wouldn't someone as thin as Asha actually vanish?' The idea brought a smile to his face.

The second portion of the note buoyed his spirits and almost caused him to dance around the table with joy. Susheela stated that she had received the report from the lab in Mysore and the results were 'positive'. She asked him to supervise the pruning of the coffee bushes in a certain block of their estate for a couple of hours, and to return home at half past twelve for a celebratory meal.

Joyappa decided that he needed room in his stomach for his special lunch, so he dumped the unappetizing porridge in the dish of Red Dog, who was lying in the garden. The dog sniffed at the congealed mess, turned up his nose and found another place to lie down at the opposite end of the garden. Joyappa was sympathetic to the reaction.

Joyappa grabbed his hat and a pruning knife before heading off to the estate. It was with a song on his lips and a spring in his step that he made his way to the part of the estate where the pruning was already in progress. He strolled between the rows of coffee bushes and concluded that the pruners were doing a fine job. He finagled a couple of beedies from a worker and enjoyed a leisurely smoke while wandering aimlessly through the estate. Then, he pulled his hat over his eyes and fell asleep in the shade of a dadap tree.

When Joyappa returned home at the specified time, he was a little perplexed to find several vehicles parked outside the house. As he entered, he heard sounds of women giggling and laughing in the sitting room. When he stuck his head around the door and peeked in, he was surprised to find several of Susheela's friends there.

Before he could sneak away, Susheela spotted him and said,

'Come in, Joy, and say hello. I asked my friends to stop by and join us in celebrating your results.'

Joyappa thought his results must have been amazingly good for Susheela to have organized a lunch in his honour. He was quite proud of himself, so he puffed out his chest, doffed his hat and said, 'Hello, everyone,' upon entering the room.

He saw Asha, of course, and averted his eyes. He also spotted the very pleasant Gangamma, as well as Mohini, Accava, Jamuna, Vinita and Anita. They all sported big smiles and said, 'Hi, Joy,' in chorus. Then he heard them say, 'Great news', 'Good job', 'Congratulations' and 'You go, guy!'

So, Joyappa bowed graciously and said, 'Thank you, ladies. It's a pleasure to see all of you,' in his most gentlemanly tone.

'Joy,' Susheela said, 'Asha and I were so impressed with the positive results in your lab report, that we asked our friends to each cook a special dish and bring it over for lunch. So, let's not waste any time and get started.'

'Mosht kind of them, indeed,' Joyappa said in a measured way, although his speech was slightly slurred due to his overactive salivary glands triggered by the strong aroma of delicious food.

Joyappa, sitting at the head of the table, was astounded by the array of delicacies prepared in his honour. Susheela and her friends clucked and fussed over him and insisted that he have the choicest pieces of mutton, the tastiest pieces of pork, the juiciest chicken breasts, the most delicious and crisp akki ottis and the largest of the fried prawns. He also gorged on the fragrant wild mushroom biryani topped with cucumber raitha and consumed vast amounts of pickled bamboo shoots.

Joyappa thought the lunch was simply magnificent and gorged until he could eat no more. The women ate sparingly as usual but were awestruck at his capacity to put away mountains of food. For Joyappa, it was the best meal he had had in a while, after being on a strict diet for so long. The only thing he missed was beer to wash it all down. When he asked Susheela if he could have the special beer from the microbrewery that she had saved for him, she replied that it would be best not to strain his digestive system in his condition. Joyappa considered it a minor issue and didn't let it detract from his special meal. After a dessert of *thambuttu* laced with warm ghee, Susheela led everyone to her study.

Joyappa waddled in last and was surprised to find the room decorated with colourful streamers, balloons and a banner that was captioned, 'Congratulations, Joy!' Susheela asked her friends to sit down and said, 'Joy, in honour of the good news, my friends wanted to give you a few presents. After all, you've been tested for years, but have never had such unusual and positive results. 'Much obliged, ladies,' Joyappa acknowledged pompously. Pride caused him to try to puff out his chest, but his bloated belly pre-empted the effort, and he wobbled a bit on his feet. Susheela invited Joyappa to the tea table on which there was a pile of brightly coloured packages. Joyappa eagerly began to unwrap the gifts.

He became increasingly perplexed as he worked his way through the presents. There were booties, bibs, pacifiers, feeding bottles and tiny diapers. He certainly felt that of all the presents could have been useful, but surely someone had erred with regard to the size.

Puzzled, he looked at Susheela and said, 'There must be some mistake.'

There was good natured laughter from most of the women. Gangamma, who had a soft corner for Joyappa, seemed somewhat embarrassed and sympathetic.

Good News!

Joyappa picked up the miniscule booties and commented, 'These are really well made but I don't think they will even fit my big toe. Do you believe there was a mix-up and my gifts have been given to someone else?'

'I don't think there was a mix-up in the presents, Joy,' Susheela said. She then handed him an envelope and added, 'I think this will help you understand.'

Joyappa opened the envelope and extracted a few sheets of paper. He saw his name and age listed on top and realized it was the report from the laboratory. He was pleased to note that for the first time in years, his levels of sugar, cholesterol, lipids and serum electrolytes were within the normal range. He nodded proudly and smiled. However, after he turned the page, his face lost all colour and he started to stutter, 'Bbbu-but, how could this be?' he asked.

The report fluttered to the ground from his nerveless fingers. Asha picked it up and said, 'Here you go, Joy. Let me help you.'

Asha cleared her throat dramatically and prepared to read the report. Joyappa seemed shell shocked as he looked at her with his mouth open.

'Girls,' said Asha, 'You will be pleased to know that Joy's pregnancy test came back 'positive'. Soon, this house will resonate with the pitter-patter of little feet again. And, Joy, in honour of this momentous, or maybe I should say, miraculous occasion, we decided to throw you a baby shower.'

Asha handed over the report along with another package to a bewildered Joyappa, who mechanically removed the wrapping paper from the gift. He held up the object and turned it upside down with a puzzled look on his face.

'Joy, I hope you find this breast pump useful. I can't tell

you how convenient it was for me, and I am sure you can put it to good use as well,' said Asha.

Susheela had planned the baby shower as a practical joke to get back at Joyappa for his behaviour in Ooty, which she considered irresponsible and embarrassing. She hoped he had learned a lesson. However, upon observing his confusion, she felt a bit contrite. So, she told her friends that she would serve coffee in the sitting room and ushered them out of her study.

Gangamma, who Joyappa considered the kindest and least snooty of the lot, didn't leave with the others. She believed that the joke had gone too far and Asha had crossed the line. She patted Joyappa on the back and said, 'Joy, it was just a silly gag. Just laugh it off and don't feel bad. I do think you should look after your health, though.'

'Thanks a lot, Gangamma,' Joyappa said, grateful to hear a kind word. 'I guess everyone had a laugh at my expense. But at least I got a super-duper yummy meal, didn't I? And now that I think about it, because everyone else ate like a bird, I get to eat the leftovers too.'

They both chuckled. Joyappa thought for a moment about the age-old practice whereby friends and relatives carry culinary delicacies to the home of an expectant mother.

'Gangamma,' he said in all seriousness, 'Our ancestors were very wise. There's something positive to be said for the tradition of providing a *koopadhi*.'

Joyappa then proceeded to examine the breast pump before asking her, 'Say, Gangamma, do you think this thing will hold booze?'

'I don't know, Joy,' Gangamma replied with a shrug. 'However, I really think you ought to cut down on your liquor consumption,' she added.

Joyappa thought about the aberrant results of his medical tests and said, 'I'm not sure how this happened.' He scratched his head and reflected on the day of the tests. After the initial shock, his brain began to function again. 'Maybe someone mixed up my samples with that of a pregnant woman,' he concluded triumphantly, with all the enthusiasm of someone who had finally solved a difficult mathematical puzzle.

'Yes, Joy,' Gangamma agreed patiently. 'That would certainly be the most rational explanation.'

Joyappa now turned his attention to the lab report. He was relieved that he wasn't 'expecting'. Yet, he felt somewhat disappointed that the 'normal' results for various metabolites were likely those of someone else, possibly the pregnant woman. He was about to discard the report, when he noticed the name and signature at the bottom of the last page, which stated 'Veena'.

'Aha, now, I know who is responsible for the mistake. When I visit that lab next, I will make sure that Veena faces the music.'

5

Dental Problems

Susheela was scurrying around all morning, busy with household chores, while Joyappa sat on his couch, reading cartoons in the newspaper and intermittently chuckling to himself. Joyappa had stayed up late the previous night watching a Hollywood movie with rather graphic content on television. The film's protagonist had been accused of committing a violent crime. Despite being innocent, the unfortunate man had been convicted and incarcerated. To add to his woes, he had been assaulted in prison, first by the warden and later by the other inmates. The unspeakable acts the poor man had to endure left Joyappa horrified. To erase the memory of the distasteful scenes that had caused him a restless night, Joyappa immersed himself in the morning newspaper.

'What's the hurry?' Joyappa asked as Susheela bustled around him.

'I told you last night, I have a dental appointment. I wish you would listen to me, Joy,' she replied.

'Good, good,' Joyappa said, although he was not really paying attention. He had finished reading the 'funnies' and was now focussed on a comic strip in which a superhero was clobbering a nasty-looking villain who had abducted his girlfriend.

'The doctor said it might be painful,' said Susheela. She was feeling somewhat nervous and half-hoped that Joyappa would offer to drive her to the dentist's clinic.

'Fine, Susheela, have a nice time,' Joyappa said with a smile as the superhero flattened the villain's henchman with a flying kick. He wondered what kind of kicking technique caused the sound '*Pow!*' to be heard.

'I will not be able to take any calls, Joy. *Do not* call me unless it's an emergency,' Susheela said firmly as she slammed the door behind her and stormed off.

Susheela's words did not register with Joyappa, although he did hear her drive away. He immediately broke off half a loaf of freshly baked bread, which was cooling on the table, coated it with butter and chomped away happily as he read the rest of the comic strips. He wished newspaper publishers would do away with the political mumbo jumbo, international news and sad stuff. Instead, he felt, they should restrict themselves to publishing sports news, weather forecasts, horoscopes and excerpts from comic books.

When he was done with the newspaper, Joyappa yawned, stretched and contemplated taking a nap. Then, he remembered that Susheela wanted him to meet the sales representative of a fertilizer company before noon. He reluctantly shuffled off to the bedroom to change out of his pyjamas into something more appropriate.

Susheela had already laid out Joyappa's clothes on their bed. He picked up the shirt and found to his dismay that it was starched. He examined the pants and discovered that they were made of some weird, wrinkle-free material. He was appalled because he knew this outfit would surely chafe his skin in the most awkward parts of his anatomy.

'I will not be wearing these awful, stiff clothes,' mumbled Joyappa to himself as he began to look for more comfortable alternatives in his closet. Like many a married man, Joyappa often had trouble finding things. Something he was looking for could be right under his nose, but for some inexplicable reason, its presence would not register upon his senses. He was now hunting for an old, faded shirt with unsightly holes near the armpits that facilitated cooling of his body on warm days. The garment admittedly looked shabby, but numerous cycles of washing and wearing had made the fabric so soft and comfortable that it felt like a second skin—albeit without the coarse and abundant hair of his 'first' skin.

Joyappa proceeded to do what he always did when he could not find something; he yelled, '*Susheelaaaa!*'

At that very moment, Susheela was anxiously seating herself in a dentist's chair several miles away and obviously didn't hear him. Joyappa bellowed her name a few times before remembering that he had heard her drive away some time ago. As he endeavoured fruitlessly to locate the shirt, Joyappa became more frustrated. He started to rant and rave. The air turned blue and caused the cats to hide under the bed but did not cause the shirt to appear.

Joyappa tried to call Susheela, hoping that she would know where to find the missing garment. The mobile phone rang and rang, but there was no response. Joyappa then dialled the number ten more times in quick succession, but again, there was no answer. Frantically, he made a dozen more calls to Susheela's second number, but to no avail.

'Women,' he muttered, angrily. 'No sense of responsibility. I have an emergency, an *actual* emergency, and Susheela is busy shopping or spending time with her friends!'

Meanwhile, Susheela was in the middle of a particularly delicate procedure. She was sitting in the dentist's chair in front of the operating lights with her mouth wide open as the dentist used one frightening instrument after the other. Despite having placed her phone in her handbag, which was left with the receptionist, its persistent buzzing was clearly audible. Susheela could tell that the dentist was becoming more annoyed each time he heard her phone ring. As if the pain and discomfort of having someone delve into one's oral cavity was not bad enough, Susheela became concerned about the repeated calls on both of her numbers—each with a distinct ring tone. For a moment, she considered answering the phone but was instantly discouraged by the dentist's scowl and stern demeanour.

Joyappa was thirsty after all the swearing and grumbling. He was pleased to discover a bottle of beer hidden beneath some jeans in his closet. As he sat down to drink his beer, he told himself that women were incredibly hard to understand. Men, at least the ones he liked to hang out with, would answer their phones immediately, and never nag their buddies with questions about their weight, food habits or personal hygiene. However, as Joyappa's annoyed gaze fell upon a framed photograph of a smiling Susheela on a beach with her girlfriends, his mood changed. He concluded that despite lacking these male characteristics, he was very glad to be married to her.

Refreshed after the drinks, Joyappa miraculously found the missing garment. It was right on top of the pile of shirts in his closet. 'How could I have missed it?' he muttered. He dismissed the thought and started to look for his favourite socks. Again, he was unable to find them. As his frustration mounted, he attempted to call Susheela several more times. Her phone would ring, but she would not answer.

Joyappa became very annoyed. He pulled on a pair of uncomfortable formal socks and grumbled when the hair on his ankles got tangled with the synthetic material. He decided to call Susheela one last time. Luckily, she responded, and he felt a great sense of relief.

'Is everything okay?' Susheela asked. Although her speech was not very clear, she sounded concerned.

'I cannot find my comfy blue and white socks, the ones with holes near the big toe, Susheela. What have you done with them? And let me tell you, you really should be more responsible and ought to answer your phone promptly.'

Joyappa thought he heard a peculiar, low pitched, angry growl from Susheela. Then the line went dead and he was left shaking his head. 'Susheela really needs to learn some phone etiquette,' he muttered.

He then drove to the neighbouring village, where he met the sales representative of the large multinational fertilizer company he was scheduled to meet. He placed an order and was pleased to receive a substantial discount, possibly because the salesman felt sorry for him after seeing him attired in a torn, shabby shirt and mismatched socks.

Susheela returned home while Joyappa was away. She was in pain and still seething over Joyappa's ill-timed phone calls. As she rested, she began to calm down. She still felt bad about the fake baby shower that she had previously organized and realized that she might have been too harsh on him. In particular, she felt her friend Asha had crossed the line. Fortunately, Joyappa did not seem to be too humiliated by the elaborate prank and appeared not to bear any grudges. Nevertheless, Susheela still felt contrite about her actions.

Susheela thought of all of Joyappa's admirable qualities—he was a good provider, cared for his family, and was unfailingly kind and considerate to his pets. Despite his often immature behaviour, she was well aware that he was loyal and certainly had her best interests at heart. *I guess I won't be hard on Joy, and will overlook his stupid phone calls,* thought Susheela.

When Joyappa returned, he immediately took Susheela to task for not answering her phone. With great restraint, Susheela pointed out that she had clearly told him to call *only* in case of an emergency. She explained that she was still in pain and his repeated calls over a trivial matter had greatly inconvenienced her and irritated the dentist.

Unfortunately, Joyappa—as was often the case—seemed unable to comprehend that he had totally ignored Susheela's instructions, and consequently caused her a lot of trouble. He was still irritated that she had not answered his calls.

'Whatever, Susheela!' Joyappa snapped childishly. 'When I really needed you for something important, you let me down. How do you think I feel?' he whined.

All of Susheela's noble resolutions of forgiveness evaporated instantly. She did not dignify Joyappa's question with an answer. *This man-child needs to be taught a lesson*, she thought.

After some contemplation, Susheela left the room and finalized her retaliatory plan. Although the dentist had not extracted any of her teeth during her visit, she carefully carved a replica of a molar out of a piece of soap. She told Joyappa that she would sleep in the guest room that night but would leave her recently extracted tooth under *his* pillow in their bedroom.

'But why do you want to leave anything under my pillow?' asked Joyappa.

'That'sh for the thooth fairy who will visit you thonighth,' Susheela answered. Her speech was still somewhat slurred and parts of her mouth were still numb from the local anaesthetic, the effect of which was yet to wear off.

Susheela explained that it was a tradition in Western countries. A child who lost his tooth milk would place it under his pillow. During the night, the tooth fairy would sneak in and exchange the tooth for a very nice gift. Joyappa had not heard of this practice before, but the mention of a gift caught his attention.

Susheela then embellished the story. She said that when a married woman loses a tooth, it is customary for her to place it under her husband's pillow and spend the night in a different room. She added that if the husband had been good, he would definitely be rewarded with a gift the next morning. Joyappa was pleased. He wondered if the gift could be Scotch whiskey or French brandy, as the tooth fairy was from the West.

'However,' Susheela warned, 'if the husband has *not* been nice to his wife, the tooth fairy can be very unpredictable, and has even been known to pull out teeth as a mild form of punishment. For very badly behaved husbands, the consequences can be much, much worse.'

Joyappa turned pale. Suppressed memories of the gruesome movie he had watched the night before came flooding back with a vengeance. He declared that he certainly didn't want *anyone* visiting him at night. Susheela, however, insisted that he should not turn down such a wonderful opportunity. She wore an innocent, wide-eyed look when she told Joyappa that

Dental Problems

as he was such a considerate and caring husband, who never lied to her, he could expect a very nice present.

Joyappa who missed Susheela's sarcasm felt caught between a rock and a hard place. It was an impossible situation. He worried about all the irresponsible, insensitive, immature and inconsiderate acts he had committed, and concluded that if the tooth fairy was aware of even a fraction of these transgressions, he had absolutely no chance of receiving a gift. Yet, he couldn't very well confess to Susheela, as her revenge was likely to take the form of a protracted cold war that would be much worse than the tooth fairy's punishment.

Joyappa was forced to pretend that he had been good. In a small voice, he said, 'Fine, Susheela. You are absolutely right. Go ahead and place that tooth under my pillow. As I am always caring and honest with you, I'm sure I will get a nice present.'

Susheela was pleased that her plan was falling into place. She wrapped the 'tooth' she had carved out of soap in a piece of paper and placed it under Joyappa's pillow.

It was a rough night for Joyappa. The traumatic scenes he had witnessed in the movie were fresh in his mind. He broke into a cold sweat when he thought of some stranger entering his room and committing horrible acts while he was asleep. In the interest of his own safety, he made *absolutely* certain that he was lying on his back, so he could keep an eye on the doorway and defend himself from hostile intruders. He also placed his loaded shotgun within easy reach, for added comfort. Yet, he was restless and sleep proved elusive. Finally, in the wee hours of the morning, sheer exhaustion caused him to nod off for about an hour. It was at this time that Susheela tiptoed into the room and exchanged the 'tooth' for a gift before quietly sneaking out.

Later that morning, Susheela breezed into the bedroom

looking fresh. 'Good morning, Joy,' she said cheerfully. 'It's time to rise and shine. I hope you slept well. Have you looked under your pillow?'

Joyappa grunted unenthusiastically. He wondered when the tooth fairy had managed to enter the room. He checked himself all over to make sure all his parts were in place before reaching under the pillow where he found a small, gift-wrapped package. Although disappointed, as it was clearly not a bottle of liquor, he was still optimistic that it might be something he would enjoy— perhaps a cigar or the DVD of the latest kung fu film.

'Oh, Joy. How exciting! Quick, see what the tooth fairy left you!' Susheela said.

Joyappa anxiously ripped open the package, but his face crumpled when he saw his 'present'. It was a note on perfumed paper, with beautifully calligraphed writing. This added to the authenticity of the message, as Joyappa assumed that fairies had excellent penmanship. The note read:

> *Beware! You must always be considerate and loving to your wife. Never, ever lie to her or you will be punished. You have been warned!*
>
> *Tooth Fairy (In-charge of southern India)*

Joyappa flung open the window, ripped up the note and threw it as far as he could. As the pieces fluttered to the ground, Susheela grinned like the Cheshire Cat. Mission accomplished!

6

The Dinner Party

Susheela was pleased with the success of her practical joke. She also believed that Joyappa deserved to suffer some more for his misbehaviour. She planned to invite her friends to dinner and enjoy the company of people who were more intellectually engaging than her spouse. She also revelled in the knowledge that Joyappa would be terribly uncomfortable in their presence.

Joyappa had spent a nervous and sleepless night. After breakfast, he started to look on the bright side; he felt grateful that the tooth fairy had not extracted any of his teeth or harmed him in any way.

As Susheela began to speak, however, his spirits plummeted. She said, 'Joy, we are having Ash, Mac and another guest over. This person is a business mogul from England who is visiting the district, and it is possible that he might be interested in purchasing coffee from this area.'

Joyappa was stunned. His insides were churning and he felt like screaming, but he maintained a dignified silence. *Asha and Machaiah!* If their company was not bad enough, he was going to have to spend an evening with a complete stranger, a business mogul (whatever that meant).

Oh, Susheela! Why don't you pull out my moustache one hair at a time; after that, bind my hands and feet and have that tooth fairy attack me, Joyappa thought bitterly.

Asha was very protective of Susheela. She tended to take offence if she felt Joyappa had misbehaved or wronged Susheela in any way. Joyappa had borne the brunt of Asha's retaliatory strikes on many an occasion, and was understandably wary of her presence, particularly after she had assisted Susheela in hosting a baby shower in his honour. Joyappa had a sneaking suspicion that Asha was the mastermind behind his humiliating experience.

Machaiah's relationship with Joyappa was also a bit strained. The reason was partly historical.

Many years ago, Joyappa's college hockey team, which included his friends Chomu and Charlie, had advanced to the final of a prestigious tournament. The opposing team, which represented a college with high academic standards, was captained by Machaiah.

Joyappa was an attacking player, a dashing centre-forward with an uncanny ability to score goals. His thick, powerful thighs allowed him to accelerate rapidly and change directions abruptly—characteristics that posed a nightmare for most opponents.

Machaiah, on the other hand, was a superb defensive player. Connoisseurs of Indian hockey praised him for his cerebral passing, positional play and finesse. The match was much anticipated as a clash between the two stars.

The finale lived up to its billing. The atmosphere was electric, as the stadium was packed with friends, family and fans of the competing teams, as well as a huge number of hockey lovers. It was a tense, evenly contested game. In the first half, Joyappa managed to score a goal after he had gathered a loose ball and charged past the opposing defence. Minutes later, Machaiah produced a brilliant 'assist' that resulted in the equalizer. Machaiah's tight marking and great anticipation meant that he intercepted most of the passes meant for Joyappa, who was growing frustrated as he could not get a clear shot at the goal. Late in the second half though, Chomu managed to thread a pass to Joyappa, who collected it and sprinted towards the opponents' goal. Machaiah however, stood in his way, perfectly positioned to make the tackle. Unfortunately for him, Joyappa abruptly changed direction. This manoeuvre wrong-footed Machaiah and Joyappa's elbow somehow made contact with his nose. Machaiah collapsed in a heap as he clutched his injured face and blood gushed between his fingers. The referees saw no apparent foul and allowed play to continue. Joyappa sprinted past the rest of the defenders and hammered the ball past the goalkeeper. His team was now in the lead!

Machaiah was led off the field, whimpering in pain from his broken nose. His absence opened the floodgates, as no one else could cover Joyappa. Frankly, no one really had the stomach to stand in his way after what had happened to their best player. Consequently, Joyappa scored two more goals, resulting in a memorable victory for his team.

After the match, Joyappa and his teammates visited Machaiah to see how he was faring. But Machaiah was sulking. He turned his back to them and refused to shake hands. Joyappa felt a bit bad at having rendered a worthy opponent hors de combat, but the collision had not been deliberate. Furthermore, it was not unusual for him to leave injured defenders strewn in his wake, and he had become somewhat inured to their plight. So, he had simply shrugged and moved on to receive the winner's trophy from the Minister of Sports and Recreation.

Machaiah had been an outstanding student. After graduating from college, he decided to pursue an advanced degree in business from a prestigious British university. He studied diligently and graduated in a short time. Armed with his international degree, he joined a multinational company with diverse business interests, including the growing and marketing of coffee. He worked hard, was paid well and rose meteorically in the firm. Recently, however, he had been passed over for a promotion and there were whispers that for some reason, the CEO of the company was not terribly happy with him. Nevertheless, he still commanded a substantial salary and held a secure position in upper management.

Joyappa was concerned about the kind of company he would have to endure during the evening, until he was suddenly struck by another thought. 'Susheela,' he said, 'as you are inviting *your* friends over, I would very much like to have *my* buddies join us for the evening. Yes, I think we should invite Chomu and Charlie to dinner.'

In the ebb and flow of the great marital chess match, Joyappa's shrewd move would have impressed even former World Chess Champion, Viswanathan Anand. It was now Susheela who felt like she had taken a blow to the solar plexus.

Oh God! Chomu! He is bound to ruin the evening with his boasting, tall stories and general crudeness, Susheela thought. She knew without a doubt that Chomu's presence would, in just one evening, leave her reputation as a superb hostess in tatters. On the other hand, she felt that Charlie, although not necessarily compatible with her invited guests, might be far easier to manage than Chomu.

Charlie was infatuated with an attractive artist named Neelamma, or Neely, for short. Neely was away in Italy studying painting and her absence had made Charlie particularly needy. Susheela had tried very hard to help Charlie mend his immature ways and make him more appealing to the young woman. However, his irresponsible habits were deeply ingrained, and Susheela often felt she was fighting an uphill battle. As Charlie was continually seeking advice from Susheela on how to woo Neely, she felt she could persuade him to behave in a civilized manner for the evening.

Other than a slight quaver in her voice, Susheela remained composed when she replied, 'I suppose you could invite them, Joy.'

'Goody,' Joyappa said happily. He hoped his friends' presence would alleviate the stress of the forthcoming evening.

But Susheela's next move was worthy of a Russian grandmaster. She said, 'Did I mention that it will be a vegetarian meal, Joy? There will be lots of salads and fresh fruit that will do you and your friends a lot of good.'

Predictably, Susheela managed to put a damper on Joyappa's enthusiasm. 'Yucky,' he muttered under his breath.

'What was that, Joy?'

'I said, "Okay",' Joyappa lied.

He stepped outside to make his phone calls. He really wanted his friends to be there to support him. So, he decided to withhold the crucial bit of information regarding Susheela's plan to impose herbivorous diet on everyone. Charlie accepted the invitation enthusiastically, saying that he wanted to discuss an important matter with Susheela. Joyappa was pleased. But he knew getting Chomu to come to dinner would be a more difficult task.

'Hey, Choms,' Joyappa said, cheerfully.

'Joyaaa,' yelled Chomu, 'What's been happening, man?'

'Oooh! Not much, Chomu. Just the usual. I hope you are not too busy this evening. I was wondering if you would be free to get together with Charlie and me.'

Chomu tended to be lonely as his wife spent most of her time in Bangalore and made every effort to avoid being under the same roof as her husband. So, it was with great enthusiasm that he responded, 'Of course, Joya. Name the place, and I will be there in no time. I've got some super rum that I can bring along.'

'Good. Why don't we meet at about six at our house?'

'Is Susheela out of town?' Chomu enquired hopefully.

'No. She is very much here. She's invited Asha, Machaiah and some English businessman over. So, I thought we could spend the evening together.'

There was absolute and uncharacteristic silence from Chomu. Joyappa wondered if he had lost the connection. Just as he was going to dial the number again, Chomu responded in a sad, weak voice, 'Joya. I'm so sorry. I completely forgot that I have a doctor's appointment. He's a specialist who is coming all the way from Chennai, so I'm afraid I can't make it.'

'What is wrong with you, man? You seemed just fine when we last met,' Joyappa asked, sounding concerned.

'Uhm. Let's see. I am having a prostate examination. It really has been bothering me of late.'

'Well, okay,' Joyappa said. He had no clue about prostate problems but was worried about his friend. He tried to be supportive and added, 'We will miss you, Choms. If your prostate is fixed, I hope you perk up soon.'

'Thanks, Joya. I would have loved to be there,' Chomu said, as he tried to sound like he meant it. 'I am sure the two of you will have fun.'

Chomu was sad that he could not meet his friends. He felt a wave of sympathy for Joyappa, and thought that should the need arise, he would gladly take a bullet for his buddy. But, having to spend a whole evening in the disapproving company of Susheela *and* Asha was the kind of trauma that he just could not endure.

After hanging up, Chomu sighed noisily and mopped the sweat from his brow. He felt somewhat guilty for having lied to Joyappa. Yet, the all-pervasive sense of relief at having dodged an awkward social event overwhelmed all his other feelings. However, his spirits were soon uplifted as he resumed the careful examination of a glossy magazine with lots of pictures and very few articles.

The house looked spotless and the garden was bursting with colour, thanks to Susheela's efforts and organizational skills. Just as she was nervously scurrying about the living room fluffing cushions and pillows that needed no fluffing, Charlie arrived. He was early, which pleased Joyappa but left Susheela a little irritated as she still had to administer the finishing touches to the evening meal.

Susheela had been worried that Charlie would appear in the mismatched, gaudy attire that he considered fashionable. So, she was hugely relieved when she saw that he was neatly dressed in a pale blue shirt and black trousers. She patted herself on the back for having dramatically improved his sartorial choices.

'Hi, Sush,' Charlie said.

Susheela gritted her teeth, as she hated this form of address, but in the interests of being civil to her guest, she managed to force a smile as she responded to his greeting, 'Hello, Charlie. You look nice today.'

Charlie was preoccupied with more important matters and did not acknowledge the compliment. Instead, he pulled out an envelope from his pocket and said, 'Sush, I've got something I would like you to see. After you encouraged me to read, I came across an article that said that chicks really enjoy poetry. I have spent days writing romantic verse for Neely and I hoped you would take a look at it before I send it to her.'

'Charlie, I have told you several times that it is not appropriate to refer to women or girls as chicks,' Susheela remarked sternly.

'Sorry, Sush. I forgot. I probably should have said, "wenches". Anyway, I think I've done an excellent job and I believe Neely will hurry back from Florence if I send this to her.'

Susheela wearily resolved to spend a few hours tutoring Charlie on an appropriate way to refer to women. But this was not the time, as she was focussed on having everything perfect for the evening. She told Charlie that his poetry would have to wait until after dinner.

Before she hurried off to perform the various duties required of a good hostess, she said, 'Fellows, you know there's someone from the UK coming over for dinner. Please be nice to him and make him feel comfortable. You never know, he just might buy your coffee if you impress him.'

'Definitely, Sush, 'Charlie said.

'Do you know when Chomu is likely to arrive?' Susheela asked, with some trepidation. In the game of thrust and parry that had preceded the evening, Joyappa had deliberately neglected to inform Susheela that Chomu had expressed his inability to attend the dinner.

Charlie said, 'I spoke with him earlier to ask if he needed a ride. He said he wouldn't be able to join us, Sush. He said it had something to do with his prostate.'

'Oh, what a shame,' Susheela said rather disingenuously. It was with iron self-control that she managed to put on a sad face and keep from skipping around the room like a little girl. Her spirits were buoyed and she felt confident that the evening would be a success. She didn't even mind that Charlie had addressed her as 'Sush', yet again.

After Susheela had left the room, Charlie whispered, 'Say, Joya, doesn't UK mean Uttara Kannada? Isn't that a district in the northern part of the state?'

'I am a little puzzled myself, Charlie. I could have sworn that Susheela said he was from England. Maybe he was born in England but has settled down in north Karnataka.'

Since Susheela had encouraged Charlie to read books, newspapers and magazines in an attempt to broaden his horizons, he had gamely tried to follow her instructions. He vaguely remembered reading something that he found curious about the English and decided to impress Joyappa with his knowledge.

'Well, I hope he is good company, Joya. Did you know that the English are said to have stiff upper lips?'

'Hmm. Interesting,' said Joyappa, 'They ought to try some of those Ayurvedic oils for their ailment. I just hope he is better company than Asha and Mac.'

The next guest to arrive was Rodney Dwyer. He showed up with a twinkle in his blue eyes, a bouquet of flowers for Susheela and a bottle of single-malt Scotch whiskey for Joyappa. Joyappa took one look at him and was greatly relieved. He guessed that anyone who arrived for dinner wearing a garish Hawaiian shirt, tattered khaki shorts and flip flops—probably picked up from a roadside vendor—was his kind of person.

Susheela blinked disapprovingly, and at high frequency, when she saw Rodney's attire. However, after he pecked her on the cheek and said, 'I thought the scenery in Coorg was spectacular, but you look so lovely that it has been erased from my memory,' Susheela simpered and blushed like a school girl. She was flattered by the compliment and the beautiful flowers didn't hurt either.

'What can I get you to drink, Mr Dwyer?' asked Susheela after their guest had been seated on the verandah.

'Oh, please don't be so formal. Call me Rodney. I'll have anything that's convenient for you.'

'We could open the Scotch you brought, Rodney,' piped up Joyappa, hopefully.

'I don't think so, Joy,' Susheela said brightly. 'I think an evening without alcohol would do us all good. I have this recipe for a non-alcoholic cocktail that I got from Asha and have been dying to try it.'

Joyappa, Charlie and Rodney looked crestfallen. They exchanged disappointed looks after Susheela had left. Rodney then casually enquired about coffee cultivation in the Western Ghats and seemed very interested in their answers.

Joyappa and Chomu explained the challenges faced by planters, who struggled to keep their heads above water due to adverse weather conditions, soaring labour costs, displaced wildlife and greedy middlemen. They could not understand how a decent cup of coffee could be so expensive in the glitzy new cafés that had sprung up all over the country, while they earned such pitiful prices for their produce.

Rodney listened keenly and seemed sympathetic to their problems. When Joyappa asked him about his life in England, he explained that he had started a computer software company years ago, armed only with his ideas. He was fortunate in that his ideas had worked, and the venture had been successful beyond his wildest dreams. After several years of running the company, he grew tired of the rat race and sold off most of the business to one of the multinational behemoths that had come sniffing around. He had retained some shares but was effectively done with the day to day running of the company. He was now 'comfortably off', travelled the world as he pleased, and was looking to invest his money in other businesses.

Rodney was toying with the idea of importing coffee from individual estates in India for sale in England. He believed that the history and anecdotes associated with particular plantations and regions would appeal to buyers in his country, and they would be willing to pay a premium for 'single origin' coffees. His computer and marketing expertise would, he believed, facilitate the process and result in greater returns to the farmer.

Susheela's appearance put an end to the conversation. She offered the men tall glasses containing a translucent liquid topped with sprigs of a plant from her kitchen garden that none of the men could identify.

'I hope you like this,' she said with a smile, before returning to the kitchen.

Rodney took a sip of his drink and said, 'Joy, old chap. Interesting concoction. I think there's a touch of coconut in the stuff along with something I can't quite identify. I must admit it quenches the thirst and all that, but if you don't mind my saying, a spot of alcohol would help immensely.'

Joyappa and Charlie were in complete accord with Rodney's sentiments. But Joyappa had exhausted his stash of booze, and Susheela had forbidden opening of the Scotch that Rodney had so graciously given him. It was Charlie who came to the rescue.

'Joya,' said Charlie, 'I've got some home-brewed *bolle kallu* in my car. It matches the colour of this stuff Sush has made. So, if we mix the two liquids, she wouldn't know we have improved upon her drink. What do you think?' he asked.

'Excellent idea, Charlie!' Joyappa said.

Charlie left on his important mission. Rodney looked a bit puzzled. While Charlie was away, Joyappa explained that traditionally, palm trees were 'tapped' and the exudate was collected in earthen pots. If this liquid was allowed to ferment, it produced a delicious alcoholic drink known locally as bolle kallu.

Charlie sneaked back with a few bottles of his special brew. He quickly poured the liquor into each of the glasses, before concealing the bottles under the enormous leaves of a *Colocasia* plant in the garden. Rodney nodded appreciatively after he tasted his spiked drink.

'What do you think?' Charlie asked, eagerly.

'This is absolutely superb, fellows. Makes me wish we had this sort of palm back in England,' replied Rodney as he wiped his mouth with the back of his hand.

When Susheela checked on the guests, she was pleased to find they had almost finished her special cocktail. Rodney told her they had very much enjoyed their drinks, while Joyappa and Charlie nodded in agreement. So, Susheela brought out a large pitcher containing even more of the stuff. After she left, Charlie doctored the cocktail and carelessly tossed the empty alcohol bottles under the Colocasia plant, fully intending to retrieve them later.

By the time Machaiah and Asha drove up in their fancy German car, the three men on the verandah had finished their drinks and were feeling a pleasant buzz. Machaiah hopped out of the vehicle, hurried over to the passenger's side and opened the door for Asha, who took his arm before walking up to the bungalow. Joyappa rolled his eyes at this overt display of chivalry.

It appeared as though Machaiah and Asha had stepped out of a glossy fashion magazine. Asha looked very thin in her expensive black dress and gold jewellery. Machaiah wore a dark blazer, with a cravat bearing the insignia of some snooty club or even snootier school. Every hair on his head was in place. His clothes were faultlessly cut; the shoes were polished to a brilliant shine; and he exuded the scent of expensive cologne and the aura of a fashion model. If the 'power couple' felt overdressed after seeing the men on the verandah, it was not apparent. In fact, it was the observers who felt somewhat shabby in comparison.

Susheela arrived in time to welcome the new guests. While Asha and Machaiah were very polite and charming with Rodney, they were somewhat cold and dismissive towards Joyappa and Charlie. Susheela suggested that they all gather in the drawing room, as swarms of mosquitoes had begun to descend on everyone.

While the guests conversed with each other, Joyappa began to feel a bit bored. So, he spent a few minutes comparing and contrasting the upper lips of everyone in the room to determine whether Charlie's claim that the English had stiff upper lips was true.

Rodney hadn't shaved for a couple of days, but his upper lip was visible under the stubble, and Joyappa concluded that it looked like a perfectly normal one. He then looked at Charlie, but no upper lip was evident under his thick moustache. Susheela was in 'hostess mode', as she smiled and engaged her guests in light conversation. So, her upper lip appeared to be quite pliable. However, Joyappa did recall that when she was annoyed with him—there were many such occasions—her upper lip could become quite stiff and forbidding.

Joyappa turned his attention to Asha and Machaiah. He concluded that Asha possessed an upper lip that actually appeared to be much stiffer than that of the Englishman's. Joyappa's scrutiny of Machaiah revealed that he was clean shaven and possessed skin so smooth that it could be a matter of envy of most women. He noticed the slight nasal asymmetry and felt a bit guilty that he was responsible for distorting Machaiah's otherwise perfect features. These feelings of guilt were, however, soon forgotten when he noticed that Machaiah had the stiffest upper lip he had ever encountered!

Despite the small sample size, Joyappa was now fairly sure that Charlie's statement about the rigidity of English lips was wrong. But what if Charlie *was* right? *That could only mean that Machaiah was more English than Rodney*, he reasoned. The whole issue was becoming too complicated and he began to feel a dull ache in his temples. He hoped that a discussion with Charlie would provide clarity to the vexing problem. He decided that this matter would have to wait as it would not be appropriate to discuss his guests' physical characteristics in their presence. Further, Joyappa observed Charlie sitting in a corner, apparently editing romantic poems, and guessed that he would not appreciate being disturbed.

After some small talk, Susheela and Asha excused themselves and went to the kitchen to gossip and giggle, under the pretext of checking on dinner. Joyappa attempted to follow the conversation between Machaiah and Rodney now that he had stopped worrying about the rigidity of the various upper lips in his house.

Machaiah asked Rodney some questions about his business.

Upon learning that Rodney had deep pockets and intended to invest in a business promoting coffee sourced from India, Machaiah appeared to focus on him with laser-like intensity. Machaiah believed that if he could land a deal with Rodney, it would be a feather in his cap and jump-start his stalled career, catapulting him to the upper echelons of the company.

In an effort to impress Rodney, Machaiah began by describing his academic credentials in excruciating detail, before launching into a self-aggrandizing monologue on his corporate achievements. Rodney nodded politely, as his alcohol-befuddled brain tried to process the information. Joyappa understood little of Machaiah's speech but was fascinated by how he managed to speak so eloquently with an almost static upper lip. Joyappa soon tired of this mental exercise and began to think about dinner. He knew that Susheela was not going to serve any meat, but sincerely hoped that she had prepared some tasty, deep-fried stuff to accompany the salad.

Machaiah began to describe the care exercised by his company while applying fertilizer, to ensure that there was minimal leaching of the chemicals and maximum uptake by the plants. He spoke extensively about the rhizosphere, macronutrients, micronutrients, foliar sprays, active and passive transport of minerals, symport and antiport of elements, transpiration pull and other topics that were of no interest to poor Rodney. These technical terms made absolutely no sense to Joyappa, who wondered how Machaiah knew such 'big-big' words.

In the midst of his monologue, Machaiah turned to Joyappa, 'I say, Joy. How many kilograms of nitrogen, phosphorous and potassium do you apply before the monsoon, old chap?'

Joyappa, who just instructed his workers to chuck a couple of handfuls of fertilizer around the base of the coffee bushes, didn't know. So, he abruptly rushed to the window and said, 'Machaiah, did you hear that? It sounded like an elephant crashing through the undergrowth. I hope it doesn't damage your new car. Just last week, a neighbour's vehicle was gored and flattened by a rogue elephant. Perhaps you ought to park it in the garage.'

This brilliant but somewhat deceitful manoeuvre brought some much-needed respite to the captive audience as Machaiah raced outside to drive his car to safety. Rodney looked gratefully at Joyappa. Unfortunately, this relief was only temporary, as Machaiah returned shortly, and proceeded to extol the virtues of coffee grown under the shade of native trees.

Rodney's eyes took on a glazed look under this onslaught of information, while Joyappa's mouth opened in amazement. Fortunately, the all-knowing Machaiah was not observing Joyappa, or he would have termed the movement of the slack jaw, 'positively gravitropic', to explain its movement towards gravity.

Machaiah's audience was literally saved by the bell when Susheela rang the brass dinner gong. Joyappa had braced himself for the vegetarian meal, but he was horrified to see there was nothing deep fried or even mildly spiced on the table. Charlie, who was unaware that Susheela intended to deprive them of animal protein, was so upset that he completely forgot about Neely's fetching smile during the course of the meal. Rodney was crushed as he had anticipated authentic Coorg dishes seasoned with a wide variety of locally grown spices. He picked listlessly at the nuts and leaves on his plate thinking that this meal was a terribly disappointing follow up to Charlie's bolle kallu, which he had enjoyed so much.

The only redeeming feature about the meal, as far as Rodney, Joyappa and Charlie were concerned, was that Machaiah's impeccable table manners prevented him from speaking with his mouth full. He did remember to compliment Susheela on a wonderful meal, but fortunately did not provide everyone with a running commentary on the advantages of a vegetarian diet, or the health benefits of flavonoids and anthocyanins. Asha quietly consumed what seemed like a few hundred micrograms of green, leafy stuff as she sipped from a glass of carrot juice.

After dinner, Asha helped Susheela clear the table and prepare freshly ground, home-grown coffee. Machaiah said he would prefer a cup of organic green tea. He excused himself to answer a call from Norway about the supply of 'monsooned' coffee, a speciality product cherished by the Scandinavians.

Rodney, Joyappa and Charlie sat by each other on the verandah. The mosquitoes had dispersed by then, and a pleasant breeze was blowing. However, the disappointment over the meal lingered, and they were unable to appreciate the ambience of the late evening.

Rodney sighed and broke the silence by saying, 'Joy, I hate to ask a personal question, but are all your meals like that? I was hoping to taste some traditional cooking with a bit of zing in it.'

'Sorry, Rodney. Not all of our meals are that boring. I think Susheela was catering to Asha and Machaiah's preferences. Quite frankly, I thought it was awful. In fact, I feel terrible that you had to suffer through that.'

'Guys,' said Charlie, 'I think I can help. I was preoccupied earlier, so I forgot to bring in the food Mummy asked me to hand over.'

Joyappa immediately perked up. Charlie's mother, Gangavva, was an outstanding, old-fashioned cook, who didn't skimp on meat, oil or spices in the name of health.

'Why don't we sneak over to my car and polish off the stuff before Sush brings out the coffee? I think she will take about half an hour, and Machaiah will probably take a little longer,' Charlie said.

Sitting inside Charlie's car, the three men made up for the nutritional deprivation they had suffered at Susheela's hands. An owl hooted nearby, but their focus on the food was so intense that they didn't even hear the plaintive sound. The tinted windows of the car were rolled up and the only light came from Charlie's cell phone.

There was no crockery or cutlery. There wasn't much time either; so, the hungry men simply plunged in with their fingers and made short work of the food. They began with flaky puffs stuffed with delicately seasoned minced meat and moved on to the pepper fried chicken that fell off the bone, before wolfing down large amounts of delicious *chillkana pandi*.

Once they were done with the meats, it was time for dessert. They devoured the very rich, *boodhi kumbla halwa* dripping with home-made ghee. As there were no napkins, they had no option but to lick their fingers clean. As it was completely dark by then—Charlie's phone was drained of its power—each hoped that the fingers they were licking were their own.

Fully satiated, the three men hurried back to the house and sat down in the living room. By the time Susheela and Asha arrived bearing steaming cups of coffee (and green tea for Machaiah and Joyappa), the three men had managed to maintain suitably innocent expressions on their faces. Susheela, who expected Joyappa to be terribly unhappy after the meal, was surprised to see a wide-eyed look on his face that would not have looked out of place on a contented baby. She sensed that he had been up to no good. However, before she could investigate further, Machaiah walked into the room with a despondent look on his face.

'What's wrong, Mac?' Susheela asked, concerned.

'I don't know, Sue,' Machaiah replied. 'I was on a call to Norway, and I believe I was on the verge of selling several containers of our "Monsooned Malabar" coffee to a potential buyer. The conversation was going well and the sale seemed imminent. So, I started to give him a detailed explanation of the manufacturing process. Not even thirty minutes into my explanation, he said he was late for a prostate exam and hung up. Now, it seems he won't take my calls.'

Huh! This prostate problem seems to be going around. I hope it isn't contagious, Joyappa thought.

'I'm sorry, Mac,' Susheela said soothingly. 'I am sure you will find someone else to buy your coffee if the person in Norway isn't interested or is unwell.'

These words of encouragement lifted Machaiah's spirits and he turned his attention to the Englishman once again. 'You know, Rodney, when ripe coffee fruits are picked, we either sun-dry them right away to produce what is known as "cherry" or remove the outer skin of the fruit by abrasion, wash the mucilage and dry it as "parchment". I must emphasize that we process both products with utmost care to ensure that the coffee we produce is of the finest quality.'

'Yes, yes, most interesting,' Rodney mumbled absentmindedly, as he wished Charlie's mother had provided even more of that delicious halwa.

'We grow our coffee under the shade of native trees, and

although this causes a reduction in light intensity and our yields tend to be lower than those of South American plantations where coffee is cultivated under direct sunlight, our methods are environment-friendly. I must emphasize that with our highly scientific methods, we average one tonne an acre of clean coffee. As I am sure you know, that is over twice the national average. I would like to impress upon you that the quality of our product is also outstanding,' Machaiah said proudly.

'Quite impressive, indeed,' Rodney said, as he wondered if he could persuade Charlie to have his mother part with her recipe for the chillkana pandi. He also hoped Machaiah's Norwegian contact—or anyone else—would call him soon, so his attention would shift elsewhere.

Then Machaiah, in an effort to either include Charlie in the conversation, or ridicule his abilities as a planter, asked him, 'Oh, Charles. What is your average production per acre, if I may ask, over the past five years?'

Charlie was comfortable and his belly was full, so he was once again thinking of Neely. He may not have even heard the question.

Machaiah tried again, 'How many, Charles?'

'Two, Machaiah,' Charlie said. One cannot be sure exactly what was playing on his mind, although it was probably not coffee production.

Machaiah was not sure he had heard right, 'Are you, are you certain, old chap? In our case, it is one tonne, which most experts consider excellent for these weather and soil conditions.'

Joyappa was not really paying attention to the conversation, but Machaiah's response suddenly reminded him of the delicious wonton soup he had eaten in a small Chinese restaurant tucked away in one of Bangalore's many back alleys.

'Yup. Definitely two,' Charlie replied, with a faraway look in his eyes.

Machaiah's face crumpled, but he was tenacious. He ignored Charlie and cut to the chase, 'So anyway, Rodney. Why don't you purchase our coffee? The quality is excellent and I am confident you will receive a positive response in England.'

'Thanks for the offer, Machaiah. I have to say you are very knowledgeable, and a veritable fount of information, but I have been considering it for a while now and would prefer to purchase coffee from private growers as opposed to a large company. This coffee Susheela has so kindly made is outstanding, so I am hoping that I can get some from Joy and Charlie.'

Poor Machaiah's humiliation was complete. Asha's face fell as well. To have her suave, erudite husband's offer rejected felt like a body blow. Her opinion of Joyappa and his friends was well known. Machaiah's unsuccessful bid was made all the more agonizing by Rodney's desire to do business with people she considered duffers.

The evening encapsulated Machaiah's recent corporate woes. He was very knowledgeable and hard working. He really should have been heading the company's operations in Asia. Unfortunately, his single-minded focus on career had caused him to become a terrible bore. His CEO, a flamboyant, fun-loving person, found that Machaiah's solemn presence cramped his style. If he promoted Machaiah, he knew he would have to frequently interact with him, a situation as unpleasant as a root canal. So, he had delayed Machaiah's promotion and had him travel to distant locations as often as possible.

The CEO was astute enough to recognize that Machaiah was a valuable member of the company. To actually get rid of him would neither be good for the company nor fair to the employee.

In addition to his encyclopaedic knowledge, Machaiah's bravery was also a much-admired characteristic.

Running a multinational company with business interests around the globe meant that disgruntled employees could go on strike, and even become violent, if their demands were not met. In such situations, top management often feared for their own safety and avoided all personal contact with labour or trade union representatives. However, Machaiah, armed with only facts, figures and a desire to get things moving again, had single-handedly waded into potentially life-threatening situations, without sparing a thought for his own safety. Typically, he would discuss the issues with the leaders of the agitation for several hours, and miraculously, the striking employees would return to work the following day. While Machaiah believed it was the data that he spewed out in computer-like fashion that helped end these strikes, his colleagues felt the unhappy workers returned to work just to stop him from talking.

The CEO may have had a low tolerance for Machaiah's long-winded and protracted speeches, but he certainly did not lack a sense of humour. He once quipped that if it were even remotely possible to grow coffee in sub-zero temperatures, he would ensure that Machaiah would be head of operations in Antarctica. On another occasion, he told the Managing Director of the company's Oil and Natural Gas Exploration division that he would gladly transfer Machaiah to her unit as he could 'bore' through just about anything.

Asha and Machaiah thanked Susheela and left in a despondent frame of mind. While Susheela was wishing them goodbye, Charlie quickly collected his empty liquor bottles from under the Colocasia plant, and hid them in his car, thereby ensuring that Joyappa would not get into trouble.

Asha and Machaiah's departure coincided with a collective lifting of the men's spirits. When Susheela returned from the kitchen after getting Rodney more coffee, Charlie said, 'Sush, remember I said I had written some poetry to Neely? Do you want to hear it?'

'Most women would be flattered to have poetry written in their honour,' she replied with a pointed look at Joyappa. 'How very romantic, Charlie! I would love to hear it.'

'I am hoping that once I send this to Neely, she will head straight back to me, Sush,' Charlie said as he unfolded his long, thin frame from a window seat and stood in front of his audience. He opened an envelope and pulled out a sheet of paper. The paper was saturated with a strong, musky perfume he had purchased from a bazaar in Bangalore that was famous for selling smuggled materials. The odour was so overwhelming that Joyappa opened a couple of windows to let in some fresh air.

Charlie cleared his throat before reading out several verses of his composition:

> 'When you are near me, Neely
> You make me all touchy and feely;
> But what I've found,
> When you're not around
> I am not as strong and steely.
>
> I must confess my biggest fear
> Was running out of beer;
> I have since grown wise,
> And now realize
> I'm terrified Neely won't reappear.

When Neely is by me, it is no fluke
That I feel very much like a Duke;
But when she travels afar,
I visit many a bar
And drink until I'm fit to puke.

Loving young Neely is risky
She makes me feel warm and frisky;
When she isn't around,
I can be found
Drowning my sorrows in whiskey.'

When Charlie paused for breath, Joyappa stood up and clapped. He thought his friend had done an outstanding job. Rodney's face was red with suppressed mirth. He had never ever heard of anyone professing his love through a limerick but was too polite to say so.

Susheela, who had expected something in the form of a romantic sonnet or a villanelle, was horrified. She hung her head in despair, worried that all of her laborious efforts could well be erased in one fell swoop. She knew she had to nip Charlie's poetic endeavours in the bud, but she didn't want to upset him.

'Um, Charlie,' Susheela said, 'your poem is very clever. Well done! But I suggest that you try something else to win Neely's heart. I do understand that some of the earliest limericks frequently referenced drinking. But all this talk of beer, whiskey and throwing up may not appeal to her. Why don't you just write her a letter telling her how much you miss her? Just keep it simple, and if you like, I can give you a few suggestions. If you feel you must use perfume on the letter, let me see if I can find something more subtle that I picked up on my travels. Perhaps, you can have some flowers delivered to her as well.'

Charlie was a little disappointed. He had spent weeks on his 'poetry'. Yet, he trusted Susheela's judgement. He said, 'Okay, Sush. I'll send some flowers tomorrow. After that, I've got to work on writing a letter that will make Neely come rushing back.'

'Very good, Charlie,' said Susheela, hugely relieved that he would not be sending his somewhat crude, perfume-soaked limericks to Italy. However, to protect his feelings and to ensure that Neely would never lay eyes upon the crude rhymes, she continued, 'I am happy you have shown such initiative in writing poetry. Why don't I keep your work in my bank's safe deposit locker, so that no one can steal your ideas?' Charlie felt reassured and smiled his assent.

Rodney had yet another cup of coffee before he chose to make his exit. He thanked Susheela for her hospitality and charmed her by complimenting her house and garden. He also told Joyappa and Charlie that he would purchase their coffee at a premium, for sale in England.

Susheela suddenly realized that she had not seen Rodney eating much. She felt guilty that her desire to cater to Asha and Machaiah, and punish Joyappa, may have caused her to neglect Rodney's needs. 'Oh, Rodney,' she said, 'I am sorry if you didn't find dinner to your liking. I should have asked you about your preferences before serving the meal.'

'Don't worry, Susheela, I have had a very pleasant evening,' Rodney assured her. When Susheela looked away for a second, he winked at Charlie and added, 'I actually ate quite well, thanks. Although on my next visit, I would very much like to taste your version of the traditional Coorg cuisine that I have heard so much about.'

'I promise to provide you with all sorts of local delicacies on your next trip,' Susheela replied with a smile.

Rodney had to take an early flight back to England the following day. He had quite enjoyed himself, and wished he could spend more time with his new friends.

As he was leaving, Rodney said, 'You must visit me in the UK. I have a house in London, a couple of country estates in England, and one in Scotland.'

'Thanks, Rodney,' Joyappa said. 'A friend has invited us to the US, and we are working on going there. Also, I just found out that one of my ancestors had quite an adventure in the Wild West, and I would like to retrace his steps. Perhaps we can visit you either on our way to America or on our journey back.'

'Fascinating!' Rodney exclaimed. 'That sounds like a really exciting adventure. I've always thought the American West is incredibly rugged and beautiful. However, you don't need to wait to visit me until your travel plans for the US fall into place. I would love to have you over any time.'

'That's very kind of you. When you visit India next, be sure to stay with us. There are so many fun things we can do together if you have the time,' replied Joyappa.

'Splendid idea!' said Rodney. 'I look forward to seeing all of you soon. Charlie, I wish you good luck with your young lady. I hope things work out for you, and remember, if you need a place to spend your honeymoon, just call.'

'Thanks, Rodney,' Charlie said. He felt slightly embarrassed but secretly pleased by the mention of a honeymoon. He was also genuinely touched by Rodney's offer.

'Cheerio!' Rodney said as he waved and drove away.

7

Joy in the Coffee Season

The 'season' in the coffee-growing areas of southern India refers to a period that begins towards the end of each year, spills over into the New Year and culminates after three to four months of incessant and frenzied activity. It is the time when the coffee crop ripens and has to be harvested. The season also encompasses myriad other activities, including picking of the ripe black pepper that is grown between coffee bushes and irrigation of the plantation, following harvest. It was that time of the year.

'Joy,' Susheela said early one morning, 'I'm sure you realize the season is just round the corner. I sincerely hope you are well prepared *this* year.'

'Hmm,' Joyappa mumbled. He felt a sudden discomfort in the pit of his stomach, which was not entirely the result of the half-bottle of pickled bamboo shoots he had polished off the previous night. The season was invariably very stressful, indeed.

'Of course, I'm prepared, Susheela,' Joyappa said nonchalantly, and quite untruthfully. 'As usual, I've got everything under control. I can't believe you feel the need to remind me about preparations for the season.'

'Well, Joy,' Susheela said patiently, while she gathered her thoughts. Joyappa braced himself as he realized he should have pretended not to have heard her, instead of responding with such confidence.

'Perhaps,' Susheela continued, 'you have forgotten about that one year you didn't recruit anyone for picking and I had to beg Daddy to send some of his workers to help us out. Maybe it has slipped your mind that three years ago, you and your pals, Chomu and Charlie, dismantled a perfectly functional engine that we needed for irrigation, and were unable to reassemble the machine. Did you *really* forget that after I insisted you fix the engine, the three of you did such a fine job that no sooner was it turned on, it caught fire and scorched a whole acre of coffee plants? Finally, we could not even irrigate the estate that year and the following year's crop was completely ruined. Then there was…'

'Come on, Susheela. Calm down. You really tend to exaggerate.'

Susheela began to blink ominously. '*Me? Exaggerate?*' she questioned in a raised voice, 'Do you really want me to enlarge and frame the pictures I took of the inferno you nincompoops set off?'

'No, Susheela, that will not be necessary. Yes, I remember the fire. You must understand that Chomu, Charlie and I, like most men, are familiar with machinery and good at repairing equipment. It wasn't our fault. It must have been a manufacturing defect,' Joyappa said as he resolved to look up 'nincompoop' in his dictionary. He had a feeling it was not a compliment.

Susheela knew that Joyappa's assertion was patently untrue. His misplaced confidence and bold-faced lie left her temporarily speechless. She was well aware that about half the parts from the dismantled engine had not been put back before Joyappa started the machine. The frequency of her blinking increased dramatically as she prepared to remind Joyappa of various other blunders that had punctuated his career as a planter.

Knowing that he was in a no-win situation, Joyappa yelled, '*Tring, tring,*' in an attempt to mimic the sound of his cell phone ringing. Then he glanced at the phone, jumped up and said, 'Important call from some people I recruited Susheela. Sorry. Got to go!' He then charged outdoors.

Susheela had just thought of another one of Joyappa's blunders: A few years before, Joyappa had wiped out several hundred valuable pepper vines by spraying them with a highly potent herbicide that he mistook for liquid fertilizer. Before Susheela could remind him in excruciating detail about the costly mistake, Joyappa's asinine efforts at mimicry followed by his rapid exit, nipped her speech in the bud.

While the season undoubtedly constitutes the busiest time of the year for coffee growers, continuous work throughout the year is required to maintain an estate. Ultimately, all of these activities, some of which are described below, are carried out with the primary goal of obtaining a bountiful crop every year.

In the low hills of southern India, situated close to the equator, coffee plants are grown under the shade of much taller trees either native to the region or introduced from elsewhere. These trees that provide shade are a vital part of the ecosystem. Not only do they shield and protect the smaller coffee plants from the intense tropical sun but they also serve to provide support or function as the 'standard' upon which black pepper (*Piper nigrum*) vines grow. Mature shade trees also serve as an additional source of income when they are extracted from the plantations for use in the timber industry.

Whereas it is critical to have adequate shade to protect the coffee plants during the hot, dry months in the early part of the year, it is equally important to ensure that there is not too much shade during the middle of the year. The sun is seldom visible during the southwest monsoon season, which normally begins in June and is characterized by months of heavy rains and grey, overcast skies. Too much shade during the rains impairs photosynthesis and can result in the loss of the coffee crop due to waterlogging and disease. It is therefore vital that the shade trees be pruned before the onset of the monsoons. This operation is conducted by skilled workers who climb to the top of the trees and remove the unwanted branches without causing damage to the coffee plants below. By the end of the year, these trees will hopefully have put out enough foliage to again protect the coffee plants from harsh sunlight during the dry season.

In addition to regulation of shade, coffee bushes need to be pruned after harvest to regulate their height and shape, remove unproductive branches and retain desired shoots. Fertilizers also need to be provided to nourish the plants; while weeds, pests and diseases must be controlled.

As with most agricultural activities, a planter could well do everything to ensure a good crop, yet the vagaries of the weather and the vicissitudes of the international markets can often conspire to make farming a frustrating proposition. Nevertheless, if there is a crop on the plant, it needs to be harvested and processed at the right time. The harvesting of the standing crop was, therefore, Joyappa's immediate challenge.

Joyappa had completely forgotten about recruiting coffee pickers until Susheela reminded him that the season was upon them. Fortunately for him, a labour contractor approached him the following day. The contractor promised to supply him with workers from another district in exchange for a small loan and commission. Joyappa accepted the offer and felt incredibly relieved because picking coffee is highly labour-intensive, and there is invariably a shortage of skilled workers during the season.

On the first day of coffee picking, Joyappa greeted the workers early in the morning. Despite suffering from a mild bout of dyspepsia, Joyappa made small talk with his labour force, enquired about their distant villages and families besides joking with them and smiling a lot. He was well aware that competition for their services was intense, and other planters would hire them in a flash, if the workers were to become disgruntled.

Joyappa had resolved to work very hard during the season, as he wanted to make enough money to visit his friend, Joe Scurlock, in America. The possibility of a trip to England to meet Rodney Dwyer provided additional incentive to do a good job. Assisted by the plantation supervisor, Joyappa spent much of the day ensuring that the work of harvesting was initiated satisfactorily.

The workers swept away the dried leaves that had accumulated on the soil at the base of the plants. Next, they spread large plastic 'picking mats' under the coffee bushes. The ripe berries were picked by hand and collected on the mats, from where they were easily gathered and subsequently transferred to sacks which were labelled to identify the individual responsible for the harvest.

Joyappa was pleased with the work accomplished on the

first day by the new employees, who seemed skilful and hard-working. As the payment was based upon the amount of coffee they harvested, the workers always tried to pick as much as they possibly could. However, Joyappa kept an eye on them to ensure they did not damage the bushes in their zeal to pick more coffee and earn more money.

The harvested coffee in southern India is typically processed in one of two ways: The simpler, less complicated method involves spreading the coffee on a 'drying yard'—or *kala*—consisting of an exposed area lined with tile or concrete. As the coffee dries under the sun, it is frequently agitated with a rake or by foot in order to ensure that the drying occurs in a uniform manner until the beans reach the appropriate moisture content—typically 11–12 per cent—which usually takes about ten days. The dried fruits are referred to as coffee 'cherry'.

The second, more technically demanding means of processing coffee that Joyappa chose to follow, requires a machine known as a 'pulper'—sometimes referred to as a 'de-pulper' in other parts of the world. The pulper is a device designed to remove the outer skin of ripe fruits by abrasion. After the skin is discarded, the coffee is fed through a 'washer', which uses water to remove the sticky mucilage that typically coats a coffee bean. The resulting product, known as coffee 'parchment', is spread out on the drying yard until the desired moisture content is obtained. If the days are bright and sunny, the parchment dries quickly and is typically ready to be bagged in about four days.

Towards evening, the sacks of coffee were loaded onto a pickup truck, which Joyappa drove to the tiled drying yard, which was about 300 feet long and equally wide. The coffee harvested by each person was weighed separately, and the weight recorded under the individual's name.

Joyappa had decided to 'pulp' his coffee to produce parchment in the hope of getting a better price than cherry coffee. So, the ripe fruits were processed by feeding them into the pulper.

Although parchment dries more rapidly than cherry, thereby freeing up space on the drying yard for processing the next batch of the crop, its production requires specialized machinery and skilled operators. Additionally, plantation owners are not permitted to discharge the waste water—resulting from the pulping and washing of coffee—into the environment as it is toxic to plant and animal life. The effluent is, therefore, stored in large tanks lined with concrete—or water-impermeable plastic—until it evaporates or decomposes. Enzymes or microorganisms are often added to these tanks to accelerate decomposition. However, if left untreated, the effluent invariably turns into a dark, viscous substance that emits a foul odour.

Joyappa, to his credit, had been responsible enough to have a large concrete-lined tank constructed to ensure that the pulper effluent would be contained. The tank was over 100-feet long, half as wide and nearly 12-feet deep. Although it had been expensive to construct, Joyappa was pleased that he was not polluting the environment. However, unfortunately, and perhaps predictably, Joyappa forgot to treat the effluent. This oversight would prove to have significant ramifications for him later in the season.

Joyappa's days were long and tiring. He typically marked the workers' attendance in the morning, supervised the picking and made frequent visits to the *kala* to ensure that the coffee was drying satisfactorily. In the evenings, he transported the day's harvest to the drying yard, weighed it and had the ripe fruits pulped.

The initial excitement of harvesting the new crop gave way to fatigue. After enduring three demanding weeks of this gruelling routine, Joyappa had mixed feelings about the season. On the one hand, a larger crop meant more money in the bank; on the other hand, he was so sick and tired of the grind that he hoped it would be over soon, so he could spend time 'relaxing' with his friends.

On the very evening Joyappa was planning to schedule a clandestine rendezvous with his pals, and possibly alleviate his stress with a few drinks, his world came crashing down. Susheela greeted him with a big smile as he got home, pecked him on the cheek and said, 'I'm proud of you, dear. You are doing such a good job that I think you deserve something special for dinner. What would you like?'

'Thanks, Susheela,' Joyappa said cautiously. Something was amiss. He was not so naïve as to believe that Susheela would cook him something special without a reason. His antennae sprang up and waved around seeking the cause of his anxiety, but he was unable to pinpoint the source.

Joyappa knew bad things were going to happen, but he did not know how badly he was going to be hit. So, he decided to make the most of the situation and said, 'That's so nice of you, Susheela. I would like some mutton pulao, with lots and lots of mutton, along with a cucumber raitha.'

'Sure, Joy,' Susheela said with a smile.

'And, Susheela, would you throw in some fried liver as a side dish, too?'

'I could do that,' Susheela responded, but the smile looked decidedly forced.

'It's been a long day, Susheela. Be a dear and rustle up a cheese, mushroom and tomato omelette right now, would you? I am *sooo* hungry.'

It took all of Susheela's will power to force out the words, 'Okay, Joy.'

Despite her best efforts, Susheela was unable to maintain her smile. As she stomped off into the kitchen, she heard Joyappa say, 'Three large scoops of pistachio ice cream should top it off quite nicely.'

Later that evening, after Joyappa had stuffed himself to his heart's content, he relaxed by watching a particularly violent kung fu film on television. Susheela, extremely worn out from her culinary activities, mopped her brow and sat next to him on the couch.

Joyappa was riveted to the screen as the leading man launched himself into the air and prepared to administer the coup de grâce to the villain with a flying kick, when Susheela innocently said, 'Joy, my mother will be visiting us tomorrow. She is attending a housewarming nearby and plans to stay for a few days.'

Susheela's words dealt Joyappa a virtual body blow. He turned ashen under his tan. There was a loud hissing sound as he gasped for air. Every ounce of pleasure he had derived from his hearty meal and the film was sucked out within a nanosecond. His lips moved, but no sound came out. An unbiased observer would have concluded that Joyappa did not harbour warm and fuzzy feelings for his mother-in-law.

Susheela had hoped that a good meal, followed by an awful martial arts movie with a weak plot, would soften the blow, but she had not anticipated *this* sort of extreme reaction. Just as she thought she might have to rush Joyappa to the emergency room of a nearby hospital, he managed to speak, 'During the *coffee season*? Who on earth visits at this time of the year?'

'Come on, Joy,' Susheela said soothingly as she stroked him comfortingly on the back. 'It is just for a week. If you are busy with coffee picking, you can spend as much time as you like away from home. You know I can't very well ask Mummy not to come. Besides, I would like to see her.'

Joyappa had inherited the genes of intrepid warriors who had unflinchingly battled dangerous foes and faced charging rogue elephants with a carefree smile. He managed to steel himself and say, 'Fine, Susheela. But remember, you may not see much of me as I am going to be very, very busy.'

Susheela's mother, Kannu, arrived late in the afternoon. Kannu was of the opinion that Joyappa was not good enough for her daughter. She felt that her son-in-law was irresponsible and possessed the intellectual capacity of an inbred chicken. Although Joyappa could be insensitive about some things, the air of disapproval emanating from his mother-in-law was typically so powerful that he knew it would be in his best interests to stay out of her way.

As Susheela and her mother were enjoying their evening tea with biscuits on the verandah, Joyappa managed to sneak into the kitchen to pour himself a cup of tea. He could see the two women chatting from this vantage point. Kannu was wearing a pale pink sari and was—as always—very well 'put together'. There was not a hair out of place, her makeup was perfect and the accessories were just right.

Joyappa heard Susheela say, 'That's a lovely sari, Mummy. Where did you get it?'

'Thanks, dear,' Kannu said. 'It was very expensive, but as I loved the colour and texture, I decided to indulge myself. I picked it up at that new boutique in Bangalore I told you about. You should shop there on your next trip to the city. They have some really elegant clothing and jewellery.'

Joyappa did not linger to hear the rest of the conversation. He pocketed a couple of cupcakes and a packet of biscuits before silently slinking out through the back door. As work on the estate was completed earlier than usual, he dismissed the employees and decided to take a very long walk before returning home.

Joyappa felt that he could use some company, so he took Lulu, his little tan and black dog, for the walk. Lulu loved these hikes through the estate. She sniffed the different intriguing odours that no human nose could detect. She tried to track wild hares, got distracted by the scent of jungle fowls, pawed at frogs, charged after squirrels and growled when she thought other dogs might be around. Periodically, she would return to Joyappa, greet him by sprinting madly in circles as if she had not seen him in ages before she resumed her activities. Meanwhile, Joyappa checked the boundaries of his property to ensure that no one was sneaking into the estate to pilfer firewood or steal coffee and pepper off the plants.

After a long and tiring walk, Joyappa made his way back to the coffee drying yard, which was adjacent to the pulping equipment and the effluent tank. Lulu's ears perked up suddenly as she spotted a night heron near the tank. She charged at the bird, and just when she closed in on it, the heron took off. Lulu lunged at the heron but missed by a whisker. Unfortunately, she was unable to stop and her momentum caused her to tumble over the edge and into the tank. The bird, on the other hand, alighted safely on a nearby *Indigofera* tree and calmly watched the dog's struggles.

Lulu thrashed around wildly, trying to swim in the dark, malodorous fluid, but she was clearly in trouble. The walls of the tank were made of smooth concrete and the dog could not get sufficient traction to climb out. Joyappa, preoccupied with thoughts of the impending meeting with his mother-in-law, was unaware of Lulu's predicament; it was only when he heard her pitiful yelping, that he realized something was amiss. He hurried to the edge of the tank. On seeing the little dog in serious trouble, Joyappa quickly stripped down to his underwear and jumped in.

Joyappa tried to grab the struggling dog, but Lulu was understandably panic-stricken. As she flailed and wriggled, he couldn't quite get a grip on her. By now, Joyappa and Lulu were completely and thoroughly coated with the thick, black slime in the tank. Joyappa eventually succeeded in grabbing the dog and hurled her out of the tank to safety. However, as he tried to climb out, Lulu became concerned and jumped right back into the tank in an attempt to assist him.

Joyappa groaned, and once again grabbed at the dog. When he finally managed to get a grip on her, he held her close to his chest, as he somehow pulled himself out of the tank and collapsed by the side.

Meanwhile, after a refreshing cup of tea and a pleasant chat with her daughter, Kannu decided to take a little walk through the estate. Timing, say great warriors and lovers, is everything. Arguably, many other factors often influence the success of any endeavour; however, timing *is* unquestionably crucial. The events that followed bear testimony to the fact that the timing of Kannu's constitutional left something to be desired.

Lulu, who had recovered by now, lifted her head and sniffed, as she detected an unusual scent. She decided that she needed to investigate the source. So, she trotted off on her mission, leaving Joyappa, who now resembled a beached whale, still lying by the side of the tank.

Joyappa did not notice Lulu's departure. A few minutes later, however, he was startled to hear a woman screaming, and the sound of frenzied barking. He roused himself and ran in the direction of the sounds. The scene he witnessed made his blood run cold. Lulu was in a friendly mood and had affectionately jumped on Kannu, as she was enjoying her peaceful evening walk. The expensive pink sari was now covered with black paw prints and smeared with dark slime from Lulu's filthy body.

Kannu no longer looked composed; her hair was in disarray and there were tears running down her face. She was screaming, 'Help! Somebody, please get this awful beast away from me,' as she kicked and struck at the dog.

Lulu, who was merely trying to be friendly, now took umbrage and began to bark at Kannu and rip off pieces of the sari as she danced around. Joyappa raced towards his mother-in-law in an attempt to stop the dog from bothering her. This caused Kannu to scream even louder, as all she could see was a huge, seemingly naked, slime-coated figure charging at her.

Joyappa didn't waste any words. He scooped up Lulu and dashed into the coffee estate adjacent to the path. He was fairly sure that he had not been recognized, so he hid behind a large termite mound and waited for his badly shaken, sobbing mother-in-law to run back to the house.

When he was sure that the coast was clear, he cautiously emerged from hiding. He first washed the dog using fresh water from a nearby drum until there was no evidence of sludge on her coat. Next, he divested himself of his soiled undergarments, tossed them into the effluent tank and scrubbed himself thoroughly before putting on his clothes. Although he was able to get rid of the adhering mucilage, the foul odour did linger.

While Joyappa led Lulu to the back of the house, he heard the sound of a car pulling out of the driveway at high speed. He put the dog in her enclosure and entered the house cautiously. Susheela appeared quite upset and was dabbing her eyes with a handkerchief.

'Hi, Susheela,' Joyappa said as he looked around. 'Where is your mother?'

'Oh, Joy!' Susheela said tearfully. 'Something dreadful just happened. Mummy just left. She was so terribly upset. She told me she had been attacked by a vicious dog and a large, naked ape-like creature! Do you know anything about it?'

'*Oh, no! Your poor mother!*' Joyappa said with the kind of wide-eyed innocence that could have earned him an Oscar. 'I haven't a clue.'

'I have seen stray dogs around, but never anything like she described. She claimed the creature had a huge stomach, and there was a terrible stench in the air as it ran towards her. It is very, very alarming. Are we safe? Maybe you need to look into hiring security guards,' Susheela suggested.

'We have never, ever had such an incident on the estate,' Joyappa said. 'I'll surely look into it, dear. I am disappointed, as I was *so* looking forward to seeing your mother this evening.'

'That's sweet of you to say, Joy. But I feel very bad for Mummy. She was seriously traumatized. It's just awful that her lovely new sari was ruined, too,' Susheela said. 'By the way, do you smell something strange?'

Joyappa didn't respond as he was already heading to the

bathroom, where he intended to soak himself in the tub along with a large quantity of Susheela's fragrant bath salts. He thanked his lucky stars that his mother-in-law had not recognized him, and fervently hoped she would never learn that he was responsible for her ordeal. Despite his relief, a small part of him couldn't help feeling hurt at being described as an 'ape-like creature'.

Following a long and relaxing bath, Joyappa doused himself with cologne until there was absolutely no trace of the evening's adventures. As he dressed for dinner, and reflected on the events of the day, he couldn't suppress a smile. He resolved to give Lulu a very special treat later that night.

Joyappa whistled happily and tunelessly as he observed the golden coffee parchment spread across the surface of the drying yard. He felt the coffee season was going very well. Prices had suddenly improved. His crop was good and the sun was shining. Bright and sunny days meant that the parchment would dry quickly, so he could bag and sell the crop at a favourable price. Adding to his feeling of well-being was the fact that his mother-in-law's stay had been greatly truncated, and no accusing finger had been pointed at him or his dog. He bent down to rub Lulu on her belly as she lay by his side with her paws pointed skywards. Lulu grunted with pleasure as Joyappa scratched a particularly itchy spot, causing her rear legs to twitch at high frequency.

A mere hour later, Joyappa's disposition had deteriorated. The wind had suddenly picked up and brought dark, intimidating rain clouds over the estate.

Rains at this time would prove to be disastrous. The first casualty of a heavy shower would be the ripe coffee on the bushes, which would fall to the ground. These fruits would have to be laboriously 'gleaned' by hand, off the soil surface, resulting in a massive increase in harvest costs and a significant decrease in 'cup' quality.

Furthermore, if rainwater were to come into contact with the partially dried coffee parchment on the yard, it would also adversely affect the quality, and ultimately the price, of his product. Rains would eventually also result in other undesirable consequences that Joyappa didn't even want to consider.

Joyappa understood that if it *did* rain, there was nothing he could do to prevent the ripe coffee from falling off the bushes. However, if it merely remained overcast, he could continue to have the coffee harvested. The major problem would be a lack of space on the drying yard because cloudy conditions would slow down the drying process and leave no room for the freshly harvested and pulped coffee.

Fortunately, there was a potential solution to the problem. Several months previously, Joyappa had invested in a new coffee dryer. Susheela had felt that the huge cost of the machinery would not justify its benefits. She also felt that sun-drying the coffee was a more environmentally friendly alternative. Joyappa had overridden her objections with numerous arguments. Whereas some of Joyappa's views were valid and did make sense, he was shrewd enough not to mention that his biggest motivation in purchasing the new equipment was to own a shiny new toy that he could play with and share with his friends.

The principle underlying the operation of the coffee dryer was similar to that of a domestic 'tumble dryer' for clothing. Joyappa's dryer consisted primarily of a large, perforated metal drum attached to various pieces of equipment. The moist coffee parchment was loaded into the drum with the help of a motorized elevator. A firewood furnace situated nearby was lit, and the wood smoke was eliminated through a long metal chimney. The heat generated from the burning wood was used to warm the fresh air inside a chamber, located adjacent to the furnace and the base of the chimney. A blower directed this heated air into the drum through a large pipe. The drum was designed to rotate slowly, thereby ensuring that the coffee would dry uniformly.

The entire structure was enclosed within a roof and walls made of metal sheets, in order to prevent loss of heat during the drying process. The long metal chimney rose up from the furnace and passed through an opening in the roof. Joyappa was particularly pleased that the chimney resembled a rocket resting on its launch pad.

It must be said that the appearance of the enormous, shiny building—about 60 feet long and half as wide—was not aesthetically pleasing, and each time Susheela saw it, she quickly averted her eyes. Joyappa, on the other hand, loved looking at the unsightly structure. Susheela secretly referred to the dryer as Joyappa's 'White Elephant', whereas Joyappa proudly thought of it as 'The Rocket'.

The looming clouds presented Joyappa with an opportunity to use his new toy, which he grabbed with both hands. With the help of his workers, he enthusiastically heaped up the coffee spread out on the drying yard, fed it to the elevator and loaded it into the huge metal drum. Dry wood was placed in the furnace, set on fire and the machine was soon humming along. By late evening, Joyappa extracted a sample from the drum and was thrilled that it was already dry. He did a little jig when he thought his workers weren't watching and went home a tired, but happy man.

The cloudy weather prevailed over the entire district during the next week. The lack of sunshine forced many estates to discontinue harvesting coffee as they could not dry the crop due to a paucity of space. Joyappa had no such problem though. His mood was buoyant, he was proud that his investment was yielding results, and even prouder that he had seemingly proved Susheela wrong.

'Well, Susheela,' he remarked one evening with his chest puffed out. 'The dryer works like a charm, doesn't it?'

'I wouldn't know, Joy,' Susheela replied. 'You are the one spending all your time in that enormous, ugly building.'

'Let me remind you, Susheela, to never, ever doubt my judgement when it comes to machinery. You made such a fuss when I wanted to purchase the dryer. Now, I think you owe me a great, big apology.'

'Joy', Susheela said mildly, 'all I said was if you take such a big loan from the bank, be sure it is a paying proposition. Or else, that huge investment would be a waste.'

'Susheela, I believe this should be a lesson to you. Instead of worrying about technical issues, you should spend more time watching soap operas or those lovey-dovey movies that you like,' Joyappa advised.

Susheela was getting annoyed, and her irritation manifested itself in some rapid blinking. Although it took immense self-control, she managed to sound civil when she responded. 'If it is working well for you, Joy, so much the better. However, we should perhaps wait until the end of the coffee season to assess whether it has been a useful venture. All I can say is that I can't bring myself to look at the structure. I am guessing that awful eyesore is over 50-feet tall, for crying out loud!'

'Okay, Susheela. Apology accepted. I must again remind you that a man typically knows what he is doing when it comes to machinery, and with your husband being a "man's man", you would do well to remember never to question me in this regard,' Joyappa said as he strutted out of the room with his chest—and behind—proudly thrust out. He was pleased to get in the last word.

Joyappa was happy that despite the cloudy conditions, it had not actually rained and he could continue to harvest his crop. Yet, the constant cycle of harvesting, pulping and drying was getting him down.

He desperately needed a break and yearned to get away for just a little while with his friends. However, due to the pressure of work and a strong desire to bring the coffee season to a close, he could not justify leaving the estate. Inviting his friends to visit him at the estate was the next best option.

His bosom buddies—Chomu and Charlie—were usually reluctant to visit his house when Susheela was home, as they could never really let their hair down in her presence. So, Joyappa asked them to meet him in the evening at the coffee dryer.

Joyappa thought his idea was absolutely brilliant. He could show off the new equipment and bask in the admiration of his friends. Additionally, he believed that Susheela would not criticize his absence from home and may actually be impressed that he was working so hard. The best part of his scheme was that Susheela avoided the dryer like the plague; so, the three pals could meet, make crude jokes and generally spend time together without worrying about being censured by her.

From the spy movies set during the Cold War era, Joyappa had learnt that undercover work required the use of code words.

He, therefore, instructed Chomu and Charlie that he would call them, mention a time and, say 'launch pad', which meant that they should rendezvous at the dryer. Their first attempt was a success; Chomu and Charlie parked their vehicles outside Joyappa's property to ensure that Susheela did not know of their arrival and sneaked into the dryer shed. Joyappa's friends were impressed with the new equipment, which made him feel proud. They made a few jokes, exchanged notes about the weather and left before they could be detected by Susheela.

The next day, Joyappa used a new code word 'Thumba', which—in keeping with the theme—is the name of a rocket launching station on the west coast of India. Chomu arrived with a six-pack of beer that they shared. The jokes became a little cruder, and the friends sang a couple of bawdy songs before they dispersed. The following day, the code word was 'Sriharikota', which referred to a different rocket launching site, located on an island in the Bay of Bengal.

The friends met every evening and as they began to party harder, Joyappa returned home for dinner progressively later every night. Yet, he was confident that Susheela had no inkling about his activities.

One fateful evening, after hearing the words, 'Cape Canaveral', Chomu brought a cooler full of beer, roasted cashews, extra-cheesy popcorn and spicy peanuts as his contribution. Charlie brought an even larger cooler filled with assorted meats, including choice cuts of pork loin, chicken breasts, gizzards and sheep liver.

Earlier that day, Joyappa had been struck by what he believed was yet another brilliant idea. He decided that confirmation of its brilliance would require practical testing. So, in addition to the rum that he had agreed to provide, he also brought several very expensive towels. Susheela had purchased the towels specifically for her mother's use. Sadly, by departing so abruptly, Kannu had deprived herself of the pleasure of experiencing the incredible whiteness, the luxurious softness and the super-absorbent properties of the premium Egyptian cotton.

As a special treat for rendering services above and beyond the call of duty, Joyappa decided that Lulu could also accompany him. The three friends and dog gathered by the dryer and locked the doors from inside. As the furnace had been fired up, it was quite warm within the building. Chomu immediately opened a few beers and handed them out. The contrast between the cool liquor running down their throats and the heat from the dryer was very pleasurable, and the friends smiled happily at each other. Lulu was given cold chicken broth that Joyappa had stolen from the fridge.

The huge metal drum, filled with parchment, made a soothing sound as it slowly rotated. In Joyappa's opinion, the sound greatly enhanced the ambience.

After he had drained his third beer, Charlie went to work. He scrounged around in every dusty nook and cranny of the dryer shed, until he found some rusty, discarded metal rods left over from when the dryer was assembled. As Joyappa and Chomu watched approvingly, he wiped the rods clean with his handkerchief and ran them through the various pieces of meat from his cooler. Chomu opened the door to the furnace and Charlie carefully positioned his ersatz skewers, so the meat would be grilled to perfection.

As they waited for the meat to cook, the friends finished the last of the beers and started on the rum and snacks. Lulu ate a few cashews, but seemed to prefer the popcorn, so the men amused themselves by tossing kernels at her and cheering, as she unerringly caught every one of them.

'Joya, that is one clever dog,' Chomu said. 'Have you thought of entering her in a dog show or have her compete in the World Canine Popcorn Catching Championships?' he enquired.

'Yes, she's smart,' Joyappa replied, 'and our best watchdog. But she is somewhat unpredictable. What if she bites a judge or chews up someone's clothes? I would be taken to task then.'

When Charlie got up to rotate the skewers, Joyappa said, 'Fellows, listen up. We have already used the furnace for more than one purpose. Not only is the coffee being dried, but Charlie is also doing a fine job with the barbecuing.'

'Hear, hear,' said Chomu.

'In keeping with this theme, I have decided that we will also use the dryer for a different, and I may add, very healthy purpose,' Joyappa said.

With a dramatic flourish, he then pulled out the snow-white towels—filched from Susheela's linen cupboard—and said, 'Gentlemen, prepare to enjoy your own personal sauna!'

He had once read that traditionally in Finland, steam was generated by throwing water on hot stones in an enclosed area, and the occupants of the room would enjoy a steam bath from the resulting vapour. Joyappa's plan was to create his own version of a sauna.

Joyappa positioned an old, wooden bench near the drum. The three men removed their clothes—but not their ultra-dark sunglasses—and wrapped the large white towels around their waists. Not wanting Lulu to feel left out, Joyappa tied a smaller towel around her, too. Joyappa then poured cold water over the heated drum, and everyone had a satisfied look as the steam enveloped them.

By now, the meat in the furnace had been grilled to perfection. Charlie administered the finishing gourmet touches by lightly sprinkling the meat with salt and chilli powder. He then squeezed just the right amount of lime juice over his masterpiece. Lulu's portion, in the interests of her health, was served without any spices or condiments.

For a long while, the only sounds that could be heard over the gentle background noise of the rotating dryer were that of chomping, gnawing, slurping and gulping of meat and liquor. When they felt uncomfortably warm in the steam from the makeshift sauna, the party animals merely stepped out of the dryer shed to enjoy the cool night air before resuming their positions on the bench.

Meanwhile, Susheela had prepared dinner at home and was waiting for Joyappa to arrive. When he didn't appear, she quickly finished her meal and decided to go out and look for him. While she was pleased that Joyappa seemed focussed on the coffee harvesting, she also felt sorry that he had been working so hard. She wondered if he might be patrolling the perimeter of their property to prevent theft and also protect them from the terrible creature that had scared her mother.

Susheela then recalled that earlier in the day she had overheard Joyappa whisper into his phone something that sounded like, 'Eighteen hundred hours, Cape Canaveral.' She was aware that he thought the chimney of the dryer resembled a rocket, and that NASA launched various objects into space from Cape Canaveral in Florida. She assumed that he might have been setting up a meeting with a technician at the dryer but wondered why code words were needed.

Susheela decided to walk over to the dryer. If poor Joyappa was toiling away, she planned to keep him company for a while. She quickly prepared a cucumber sandwich. She felt that if he was in the middle of something critical and could not return home for dinner at a reasonable hour, he would appreciate a snack.

As Susheela approached the dryer shed, Lulu—the only sober participant in Joyappa's festivities—heard her footsteps and let out a low growl. The door had been inadvertently left ajar after Chomu had returned to the shed after stepping out to cool himself for the third time.

Charlie, who happened to be standing close to the door, peeked out upon hearing Lulu's warning. 'Guys, I see someone coming! *I think it's Sush!*' he said in an urgent whisper.

Joyappa, chewing noisily on a piece of pork, didn't hear the warning. Charlie did not want to be in Susheela's bad books, so he grabbed his clothes and desperately launched himself towards a small, horizontal gap between the wall and the floor that he spotted at the far end of the shed. Despite his enormous appetite for unhealthy foods and liquor, Charlie, much to the amazement of his friends, was extremely thin. Consequently, he managed to wriggle through the gap and exit the building. Lulu also squeezed her way out through the same opening.

Upon hearing Charlie's warning, Chomu panicked. He was terrified of Susheela and wished to avoid a tongue-lashing. Consequently, he made an ill-advised dive towards the same escape route that Charlie and Lulu had used. He rolled over onto his back and tried to wriggle out to safety. Unfortunately for Chomu, his large paunch—made even larger by the recent bout of uncontrolled eating and drinking—got stuck. His head and chest made it through the gap, leaving the rest of his desperately squirming body within the shed.

When Susheela entered the building, she was shell-shocked. The cucumber sandwich fell to the floor from her nerveless fingers. She observed Joyappa, wearing his dark, almost opaque, sunglasses and swigging rum directly from a bottle. His moustache was smeared with animal fat, which had dribbled down his chin and coagulated on the thick hair that blanketed his chest. There was a once-white towel around his waist.

Joyappa had not noticed Susheela in the doorway. As she watched in disgust, he stood up, picked up a bucket of water and threw it on the heated drum of the dryer. He then stood close to the drum and raised his arms. He was disappointed to find that his body was not enveloped in steam. Upon reflection, he concluded that the drum was not hot enough, and he would have to feed the furnace with more wood.

Susheela then sensed some movement at the opposite end of the shed and was horrified to see two hairy, wiggling legs and an enormous stomach trapped in the gap between the wall and floor. Seeing one of her expensive towels wrapped around that stomach added to her revulsion.

She looked around and observed the remnants of barbecued meat and empty liquor bottles. She quickly determined what had transpired before her arrival. As she stared at Joyappa, the hairs on his body stood up. He sensed he was being observed and turned towards the door. He was so stunned to see his wife there that he almost collapsed.

Susheela glared at Joyappa for a whole minute. It was an intense look of such fury that Joyappa's blood ran cold. She pointed to Chomu's wriggling legs and said, 'After you get rid of that ghastly creature, Joy, burn the towel that is wrapped around it. I suggest you spend the rest of the night right here in this hideous building as I am locking all the doors to the house. You may, if you choose, return in the morning when I will discuss this matter with you in great detail.'

When Charlie and Lulu were sure that Susheela had left, they sneaked back inside. Joyappa and Charlie managed to extricate Chomu after much effort. Lulu and Charlie sat on Chomu's swollen belly to compress it, while Joyappa tugged at his legs until he was finally free.

Chomu and Charlie left in a sombre mood. After all, bosom buddies sense each other's pain. They were well aware that Joyappa was in for a monumental dressing-down. Joyappa, however, decided to make the best of a bad situation. He put more firewood in the furnace, threw some more cold water on the dryer, finished a half-eaten piece of chicken and the cucumber sandwich that he found on the floor, washed it down with the last of the rum and settled down to sleep on the bench with Lulu by his side.

Joyappa woke up the following morning feeling sore and miserable. He put Lulu in her enclosure before he went to the house and knocked on the door. He was in a pensive mood. He reflected that he had been literally caught with his pants down; so, his usual strategy of obfuscation, half-truths, outright lies and feigned loss of memory would not get him out of trouble. He decided that he wouldn't respond verbally, regardless of what Susheela said to him. If Susheela said something particularly harsh, he would act like it actually pained him physically. He hoped that this tactic would instil some measure of compassion in her.

Susheela kept him waiting for a while before she opened the door. Her face was expressionless and she just looked coldly at him for several minutes. This silence made Joyappa uneasy, so he started to shuffle towards the bedroom.

'Not so fast, Joy,' Susheela remarked to stop him in his tracks. 'I am really disappointed in you. I cannot understand why you behave in such an immature manner.'

Joyappa winced. He hoped Susheela would think it was her words that truly hurt him.

'I thought you were doing particularly well this year. We seem to have a good crop and you were working so hard. What has gotten into you?'

Joyappa nearly responded that it was beer, rum, popcorn and lots of delicious meat that had 'gotten into' him. In the nick of time, he realized that the question was rhetorical, so he maintained a stoic silence.

'I think I know what happened,' Susheela said. 'It was that disgusting pal of yours, Chomu, who probably led you astray.'

Joyappa flinched as if he was in physical pain. Rather than eliciting any sympathy from Susheela, his body language and silence seemed to enrage her.

She shuddered involuntarily as she recalled the still-vivid image of Chomu's semi-nude lower body flapping around on the floor. She somehow managed to suppress this mental picture and steeled herself to continue with her lecture, 'I wish you would spend more time with Charlie instead. In the past, I used to think he was totally out of control. After he told me he was interested in marrying Neely, and I began to guide him towards this goal, he started to behave much better. He has stopped smoking and drinking, and is a much more responsible person these days. If he continues to follow my advice, he might actually transform into good "husband material".

Joyappa kept his counsel. He couldn't possibly betray his pal, the man who had so thoughtfully provided everybody, including Lulu, with perfectly grilled meat last evening.

'I was happy for you when the coffee dryer seemed to be working. You asked me not to get involved because you claim to be so skilled with machinery. But I would like to inform you, as you seem to lack a fundamental understanding of science and for that matter, basic common sense, that if you keep pouring water on something you are trying to dry, it just *isn't* going to dry. You may have noticed that the enormous drum containing parchment is perforated.'

Susheela noticed a puzzled look on Joyappa's face. She realized that words with more than two syllables often had that effect on her husband.

'I meant the drum has holes. Much of the water you poured on the drum to create your sauna would have entered it and been absorbed by the coffee inside. So not only have you slowed down the process of drying, but re-wetting the partially dried coffee would also have reduced its quality. Did you even consider that factor before you embarked on your stupid, irresponsible plan?'

Joyappa had been so pleased with the way his sauna had worked that he had not considered 'that factor'. He decided that he couldn't take this dressing-down any longer. So, he opened his eyes wide and tried to adopt the sorrowful expression that dogs wear on their faces when they are being disciplined for digging up the garden or gnawing on the furniture.

Susheela, however, seemed to be unaffected by his dejected look as she established the rules for the next few weeks. 'From now on, you will focus entirely on finishing the harvest. The weather has cleared up and the meteorological department says it is going to be bright and sunny for the next three weeks. So, I want you to dry the coffee on the yard. Drying the coffee in the sun is a more environmentally friendly approach. Your shiny new toy may be useful in cloudy weather, but it consumes far too much firewood and diesel to justify its use when there is adequate sunshine.'

Joyappa was eager to take a shower. The pork fat congealed

in his chest hair had begun to cause an itchy sensation and he felt a desperate urge to wash it off. As he slowly walked towards the bathroom, he heard Susheela say, 'After the coffee is harvested, you had better concentrate on having the pepper picked. And after that, if we don't get "blossom showers", you will have to irrigate the estate, so we can actually harvest a crop next year.'

'Fine,' Joyappa said wearily.

'Oh, and there is one more thing I wanted to ask you, Joy,' Susheela stated.

Joyappa turned around slowly wondering just how much longer this lecture would continue. He restrained himself from scratching his chest.

'It is about what happened to Mummy,' said Susheela.

Joyappa's heart began to pound so hard that he was worried Susheela would see it thumping against his chest. He hoped the pork fat would keep his torso immobile. To his credit, Joyappa's demeanour remained unaltered as Susheela studied his face with the intensity of a scientist scrutinizing a specimen under a microscope.

'That yappy little dog that follows you around like a shadow is a consummate troublemaker. So, I was wondering if you and Lulu had anything to do with Mummy being attacked the other day.'

Joyappa knew he was on thin ice. He knew that his happiness and, indeed, the very foundation of marital harmony were under serious threat. Every iota of histrionic ability from every cell of his body would have to be summoned.

Joyappa rose to the occasion. 'Susheela,' he said calmly, and with great dignity. 'I deeply resent the accusation. That poor animal is the best watchdog on our property. Should you be blaming Lulu for attacking a much-loved member of the family? I am disappointed in you, Susheela.'

Susheela continued to intently examine Joyappa's face and body for inadvertent twitching, lack of eye contact, sudden fidgeting, changes in skin colour, facial tics and other indications that he might be lying. Despite her best efforts, she was unable to discern any of the classic symptoms that cause master interrogators to say, 'Aha! That person is fibbing. Let us investigate this matter further!'

'I have been working hard and all I was doing was letting off some steam,' Joyappa said. Susheela considered if he was trying to be flippant, before deciding that he was quite serious.

'Honestly, do you actually believe that I would frighten away my very own mother-in-law? Come on, Susheela, I feel so hurt and saddened by what you said. I would never, ever inconvenience someone as lovable as your mother. And do you really believe that poor Lulu, who would not harm a fly, actually *attacked* your mother?' Fortunately, his nose did not elongate with each lie.

Sadly, there were no witnesses to Joyappa's masterful performance. The finest thespians would have appreciated his efforts. Meryl Streep would have complimented his stellar performance in an impeccable Indian accent; Shabana Azmi might well have shed copious tears of appreciation; while Marlon Brando would have surely mumbled his approval if they had had the privilege of observing his superb acting.

Joyappa sounded so convincing that Susheela began to actually feel ashamed about hurling unjust accusations at him. She resolved to give Lulu a juicy bone that evening. In a small, guilty voice, she said, 'I just thought I would ask, Joy. I am sorry if I hurt your feelings.'

Joyappa nodded graciously and, maintaining a sad look on his face, entered the bathroom. Upon closing the door behind him, he let out a huge sigh and almost collapsed with relief at his narrow escape.

Joyappa spent the next few weeks finishing up the coffee harvest. It had been a hectic and gruelling time. As the last coffee bush on his estate was being picked, he felt a strange sense of emptiness. He was beset with conflicting emotions—pleased that he was done with coffee picking, yet somewhat dejected that there was no more coffee to harvest.

Now that the coffee was picked, it was time for Joyappa to turn his attention to the pepper crop. Once the last of the coffee had been dried and bagged, the drying yard was swept clean to make place for the freshly picked pepper.

Black pepper provides coffee-growing farmers in South India a welcome additional income. The black pepper vines—planted at the base of the tall shade trees—cling to these tree trunks for support while growing upwards. The shade trees also provide food and shelter to a variety of animals, birds and insects. So, a well-maintained plantation forms a relatively balanced and biologically diverse ecosystem.

Joyappa now needed workers who were skilled at scaling trees and harvesting the pepper crop without damaging his vines. He couldn't just hire anybody for the purpose. Luckily for him, Chomu have him a call and said he had a number of workers from Kerala who had just completed his pepper harvest and were looking for work. Joyappa gladly hired them.

Work proceeded smoothly. During the course of the pepper

harvest, Joyappa felt the urge to fire up the dryer to process the pepper as an excuse to have another get-together with his friends, but he managed to restrain himself. Finally, the pepper was harvested, sun-dried, weighed and kept in storage, where it would remain until prices rose to a suitable level. The workers were efficient and the entire process was completed in three weeks.

The weather at this time was brutally hot. The skies were clear and the tropical sun beat down mercilessly on the district. The flower buds on the coffee bushes had elongated and were poised to bloom. However, the plants needed rain for the flowers to open. Without adequate moisture, the buds were likely to turn pink and dry up, which would be catastrophic as it would result in the failure of next year's crop.

With no clouds in the sky, Joyappa decided to irrigate the estate and artificially induce flowering. Much of the rainwater during the monsoon had been directed towards a large tank situated in a low-lying area. Using a powerful diesel engine, coupled with a water pump, Joyappa planned to irrigate his estate with overhead sprinklers. However, first, he wanted to service the engine as it had not been used for a long time.

The easiest option was to ask a local mechanic to carry out the task, but Joyappa's ego prevented him from doing so. Instead, he decided to enlist Chomu and Charlie to help him change the engine oil, irrigate the estate and show Susheela just how proficient he was with the maintenance and operation of machinery.

'Choms,' Joyappa said over the phone, 'why don't you come on over for a while.'

'Joya, you cannot be serious,' Chomu replied. 'Do you honestly think I want to see Susheela again?'

'Well, you didn't exactly see her, did you? It was *she* who saw you in that embarrassing position,' Joyappa said with a laugh.

Susheela had appreciated Joyappa's diligent efforts to complete the harvest and treated him with slightly more warmth than she had exhibited soon after the dryer fiasco. Consequently, his mood was upbeat.

'She actually referred to me as "that ghastly creature!" That was not at all nice, Joya,' Chomu whined.

'Look, Chomu. I just wanted to ask you and Charlie to help me change the oil in my irrigation engine. These local mechanics don't know what they are doing, so I thought the three of us could finish the job in a jiffy. Moreover, Susheela never comes down to visit the area where the engine is seated, so we could work and have a couple of beers. What say you, my friend?'

'If you are sure that I won't encounter Susheela, I have to say that it is a fine idea, Joya,' said Chomu as he parked his sunglasses on his head and thrust his prominent lower jaw even further forward. 'You are right about those mechanics. I've forgotten more about diesel engines than any mechanic or engineer knows.'

'Okay, Choms. Would you pick up Charlie, several litres of diesel and some engine oil? It would be best to get Castrol oil for diesel engines. I can just check and tell you which grade if you can wait a minute,'

'No, you do not have to tell *me* what kind of oil I need to bring, Joya. I just told you I'm an expert on engines. I will get Charlie to buy some fuel and the right kind of oil before I pick him up. Do you think I should bring some hard liquor with the beer?' Chomu asked.

'Nah. Let's just stick to beer,' Joyappa suggested. The irrigation tank was deep, and in the interests of safety, he did not want his friends to get sozzled on hard liquor while working by its side.

The three friends met by the engine, and after chugging a few beers, Chomu and Joyappa got to work. Charlie seemed preoccupied and kept jotting down something in a small notebook.

'Hey, what are you doing, Charlie?' Joyappa asked.

'Oh, nothing much, Joya. I miss Neely, and I was writing some poetry. You know, she has such beautiful skin. It's as smooth as glass. Can you think of a word that rhymes with "glass"?'

Chomu, who was in the middle of draining the old engine oil, chuckled and said, 'I can think of a great word, Charlie.'

'Okay, that's enough, Choms,' Joyappa said, anticipating an inappropriate comment. 'Charlie, why don't you give it a rest for now. There will be plenty of time for your poetry later. Please fill the fuel tank and hand me the new oil that you just brought.'

'Sure, Joy,' Charlie said. He dutifully topped up the fuel tank as requested. Then, he broke open the seal of a large can and handed it to Joyappa.

Joyappa was relieved that there were no parts remaining after they had reassembled the various bits and pieces of the engine. The engine was wiped down until it was gleaming, and the three friends rested for a while as they smoked. They were pleased with their efforts, and confident that the engine would purr like a kitten. After a while, they decided that before connecting it to the irrigation pipes, the engine needed to run for a few minutes.

Joyappa fitted a charged battery to the engine and hit the 'start' button. The engine started immediately. The friends smiled and applauded themselves for their competence. Soon, however, the machine started to cough and sputter. Within a few minutes, it came to a complete stop, and the only sound they could hear was the gentle cooing of a dove.

Joyappa made numerous attempts to get the engine to run again, but it refused to start. He scratched his head and asked, 'Chomu, are you sure you brought the right oil?'

'I asked Charlie to pick up a large can of Castrol 15W-40 oil for diesel engines. Where's the empty can, Charlie?' said Chomu.

'Here it is, Choms. Take a look at the label if you like,' Charlie replied as he tossed the can to him.

'Oh God!' Chomu said as he read the label on the can. Charlie had somehow managed to botch the simple task he had been assigned. The label on the can read:

> 'Castor Oil with additives
> For oral and topical use.
> Take a spoonful and feel the flow
> Or rub it all over for a healthy glow'

'What have you done, Charlie? This is the wrong stuff!' Chomu yelled. After he recovered from the initial shock at the careless mistake, a thought crossed his mind that the person who had written that awful slogan had the same poetic sensibilities as Charlie.

'I hope you've poured in diesel and not something else,' Joyappa asked, sarcastically.

'It was petrol, fellows. You asked me to fill the fuel tank. So, I filled the tank with fuel. Now, stop asking me silly questions. I've got important things to do,' Charlie said, somewhat annoyed. He was more focussed on trying to complete a poem about Neely's alluring features, with special emphasis on the texture of her epidermis. He seemed unperturbed that the petrol he had introduced into Joyappa's diesel engine had probably ruined it. Instead, he gazed at the horizon as he pictured Neely's face and struggled to find a word to rhyme with 'pores'. This time, he didn't ask his friends for help.

Joyappa was livid. As Susheela was so fond of pointing out, he had previously worked on an engine with Chomu and Charlie, and their overconfidence had wrecked the machine and resulted in a fire. This time, everything had seemed to go smoothly and he had been sure of redeeming himself. Now, thanks to Charlie's romantic preoccupation, Susheela would have one more 'incident' to hold over his head. Chomu had to physically restrain Joyappa from weighing down Charlie with a rock and dropping him into the deep end of the tank.

'Sorry, Joya. It was an honest mistake,' Charlie said after he made an entry in his notebook. He did not seem particularly contrite.

The engine was most likely, badly damaged. Worse, all the mechanics in the area who Joyappa contacted were too busy to come at short notice. With not a single cloud on the horizon, a crisis was brewing in Joyappa's life. He urgently needed to irrigate his estate if he wanted to harvest a good crop next year. Besides, if Susheela discovered that the collaboration with his friends had ruined yet another engine, there would be hell to pay.

For the next three days, Joyappa desperately tried contacting a number of mechanics. Every single one of them said, 'Sir, I am busy at the moment, but I *guarantee* I will come tomorrow.'

Every day, Joyappa waited anxiously for the arrival of someone who could get his engine up and running, but no one showed up. To add to his tension, Susheela kept asking him how the irrigation was progressing.

Joyappa responded to Susheela's queries with a confidence

he did not feel. Borrowing from his mechanics' approach, he put on a positive, if inaccurate, spin on things, 'I *guarantee* that we will have a great crop next year, Susheela. Don't concern that pretty little head of yours with irrigation. Everything is under control. I don't think you should go to the area we are sprinkling, though. I've spotted a whole family of Russell's Vipers there, and they are quite aggressive.'

'Okay, Joy,' said Susheela, 'I am glad things are progressing on schedule. You had better be careful around those snakes.'

Short of water, the coffee and pepper plants began to show symptoms of stress. Joyappa felt more pressure to irrigate the estate before Susheela found out about his blunder.

Joyappa was so desperate that he ultimately devised a wild and patently illegal plan. He decided to abduct a mechanic, blindfold him and demand that he repair the all-important engine. The victim would be released only after the sprinklers were up and running. Joyappa intended to pay the man three times his normal fee and release him from where he had been picked up—so there would be no hard feelings.

Joyappa shared his idea with Chomu, but left Charlie out of the loop, as he believed the latter's obsession with romantic verse would impair his effectiveness. Unsurprisingly, Chomu was keen to go ahead with the plan.

Neither Joyappa nor Chomu appeared to be daunted by the illegality of their venture. They also seemed unconcerned about a critical part of their plan; namely, how they would prevent the mechanic from pressing charges against them. Perhaps, they imagined that their victim would be afflicted by 'Stockholm syndrome', thereby causing him to bond with his captors and enjoy a drink with them after he completed his work. It is also entirely feasible that they expected the poor mechanic to repair their engine while blindfolded, so his abductors would remain unidentified.

The following day, Joyappa waited until Susheela had left for one of her social work projects to assist underprivileged children. Sitting in his bedroom in his pyjamas, Joyappa started to accumulate the materials for his master plan.

He decided that as he didn't have handcuffs, he would use the *laadi* of his pyjama bottoms to tie up the mechanic's hands. So, he yanked out the string, and his pants promptly fell to his feet. Looking down, he realized that his briefs could be cut up to fashion a blindfold. But his white underwear would not serve the purpose. In most of the movies he had seen —it must be said they were 'B' movies—never had he observed a white blindfold.

Joyappa desperately looked around for a blindfold. He thought Susheela might have something suitable in her wardrobe—after all, she seemed to have lots of clothes. He rummaged through her bureau until he found a piece of black cloth. 'Aha!' he yelled happily as he carefully examined its dimensions. 'This should be perfect!' In his excitement, he did not think of the consequences of filching Susheela's bikini top and using it for his hare-brained scheme. But Joyappa was not done. He wanted his plan to be foolproof. He decided he now needed something to keep the mechanic from screaming. So, he searched his pile of unwashed laundry until he found something appropriate. *Now, we're talking*, he thought somewhat incongruously, as he held up the socks he planned to use as a gag.

He began to hum to himself. His plan was coming together; and he was of the opinion that the abduction of the mechanic should be carried out late that very evening. As he picked up his phone to call Chomu, he heard a rumble overhead.

Joyappa peered out of the window and looked skywards. He was thrilled to find dark clouds blanketing the sky. The weather had changed dramatically overnight, and it seemed like rain was imminent.

Joyappa pulled on a T-shirt and shorts and ran outside. As he stepped onto the lawn, an enormous raindrop fell on his head. Gradually, more and more drops began to fall. The heavenly scent of the first shower of the year permeated the air. The raindrops formed large bubbles when they hit the ground, and Joyappa remembered that an old worker had once told him that such bubbles were a harbinger of a heavy shower. He hoped the clouds would not be blown away by the wind—insufficient rainfall would cause the flower buds to dry up. But he need not have worried; the intensity of the rain increased and soon, the parched earth was soaked.

Joyappa was confident that the 'blossom shower' would result in healthy flowers and a good crop. Moreover, Susheela would never come to know about the fiasco with the irrigation engine. He was so relieved that he began to dance in the rain. His thin shirt left little to the imagination; and as the vigour of his dancing increased, so did the jiggling of his body parts.

Several of the estate workers had been busy pruning coffee bushes nearby. When the rain started, they took shelter under the pepper vines. As they huddled together, they were pleased to see their employer being magically transformed from a tense, grumpy ogre into a happy, childlike person.

Although Joyappa would not have won a 'Wet T-shirt Contest', it is probable that the sheer unadulterated joy of his performance would have garnered at least a vote, or two, from the judges. The dogs became excited and began to chase after him. When he tripped on the slippery grass and went down in a heap, they were all over him; Lulu licked his face, Sphincter danced around him, Bean raised her head and howled, Red Dog barked happily and White Dog sat on his chest. The cats, as they calmly watched the drama from a window in the house, began to purr.

Susheela returned early because of the rain. She stopped at the base of the driveway to observe the frenzied activity on the lawn. Even as she saw a bed of her carefully tended pansies being destroyed, she couldn't help smiling at the joyous scene in the garden.

Acknowledgements

I am grateful to Yamini Chowdhury of Rupa Publications for her support in the publication of both this novel and its predecessor, *Joy in Coorg*. I also thank the editors and the Rupa team for their efforts. I believe that the editorial work and incisive questions of Aasha Gulrajani Swarup have enhanced this book, and am very grateful for the same. I remain indebted to Patricia Taylor for her steadfast support, encouragement and constructive criticism during the writing of this novel.

Glossary

Akki otti	Flat bread made from rice, often served soon after being heated over charcoal embers
Bolle kallu	Alcoholic beverage obtained after 'tapping' palm trees
Boodhi kumbla halwa	Sweet dish made from ash gourd
Chillkana pandi	Dry, often spicy, pork dish
Kala	A large and open area that is used to sun-dry coffee. Typically, the surface of such a 'drying yard' is made of concrete or terracotta tile to facilitate drying.
Koopadhi	Delicacies traditionally taken to the house of a pregnant woman by relatives or close friends in Coorg
Laadi	Drawstring. String used to fasten pyjamas (or old-fashioned boxer shorts) around the waist
Monsooned Malabar	Specialty coffee produced along India's Malabar Coast by post-harvest processing of coffee beans during exposure to monsoon winds from the Arabian Sea
Pandi curry	Traditional Coorg dish consisting

	of curried pork and flavoured with various roasted spices, and a special, dark vinegary extract (*kachampuli*) made from *Garcinia* fruit
Thambuttu	A sweet dish made from ripe bananas